A
RAGGED
PLOT

Books by Richard Barth

THE RAG BAG CLAN
A RAGGED PLOT

A RAGGED PLOT

RICHARD BARTH

The Dial Press New York

Published by
The Dial Press
1 Dag Hammarskjold Plaza
New York, New York 10017

Manufactured in the United States of America

First printing

Library of Congress Cataloging in Publication Data

Barth, Richard, 1943–
A ragged plot.

I. Title.
PS3552.A755R3   813'.54   80-25878
ISBN 0-8037-0053-9

To my parents,
Otto and Felice Barth,
with love

1

HE was thinking about Jacob's blintzes when he felt the gun in his side. At first he mistook the pressure for that twinge of heartburn that came after a session with three of the over-fried, overstuffed lumps Jacob called blintzes. Such a disgrace, he always thought, especially for one of the best *glat* kosher restaurants in the district. Next time he'd try the kasha varnishkas and leave the blintzes for someone with a better stomach. He put his free hand up to his chest to rub the heartburn away and recognized the steel of the barrel and froze.

"Don't move!"

He stared straight ahead at the chrome elevator doors that were just beginning to open. Such a schlemiel, he thought. Keep your mind on business, not on blintzes. How many times had he told his son never get on an elevator before checking it out first. He looked up. Especially one without TV surveillance. He gripped the valise tighter and waited. Run? At my age? he thought. Let them have it. Then he remembered Manny, his insurance broker. God, what a field day he's going to have with next year's rates. Shmuck! He shook his head.

The doors opened fully, and he felt a hand pushing him out. Not a shove, just a gentle, convincing force. The hand guided him down the empty corridor to the right, then into the alcove by the freight elevator. A sixty-watt bulb barely illuminated the gray walls and chicken-wire glass of the doors. There was only one of them, he thought. He could tell from the sound of the footsteps, but as yet he hadn't seen anything.

"Okay, Pop. Face the wall. Hands out."

He did as he was told. He was an old pro at this already. His third robbery. Not a bad record for forty-two years peddling precious stones. Only this time was different: this time was not for *bubkes* like the last one when he was carrying some cheap colored spinels with only a few papers of diamonds mixed in, or like the first time over twenty years ago when he was finishing a day and had only a few karats of melee left. But not today. Today he was hot, over $250,000 in cut stones, first quality. It's what happened when people got to know you at the Diamond Dealers Club: they trusted you with better merchandise. That's why he had to get a little peek. All he had so far was the impression of one person and the memory of a heartburn.

The valise was attached to his wrist with a link chain and handcuff. He thought he'd be asked for the key and then he'd grab a look, but immediately he felt a slight pressure against his wrist, and then heard the chain snap.

"Okay, drop it!"

Bolt cutters, he thought, and felt himself release the handle.

"Stay that way!"

It occurred to him that he hadn't said one word during the entire holdup, not even the simplest sound of surprise. I must say something, he thought anxiously. I can't let this happen as though I were some deaf-mute. Before he knew it, he was turning around, his mouth just beginning to open.

He would tell Manny about it a week later, after he was released from the hospital . . . about the light flickering and the floor spinning up toward him, and the tiny stars exploding around him like confetti at his nephew's bar mitzvah. What he wouldn't tell Manny, though, was the peculiar impression he had just before he blacked out.

They found him on the floor of the alcove with a six-inch section of chain still connected to his wrist and a lump on his head the size of the famous Koh-i-noor. His name was Rosenblatt, and the robbery would become the second largest of New York's diamond district since the Tal case.

2

MARGARET Binton secured the little flowery hat on her head against the light breeze and walked out of her building. She had guessed right. Her gray woolen shawl was just right for the mild weather. She turned around and smiled through the door at the white-haired elevator man. Then, before turning away, she stole a look at her reflection in the glass. The shawl even looked nice with her new spring pocketbook, although . . . She swiveled a little to the side. Yes, maybe the bag was a little too big for her. Never trust those salesgirls. Oh, well, it was done. She passed her hand along the side of her gray head to make sure her bun was in place, then headed toward Broadway.

As she reached her corner and the vegetable stand, she quickened her pace. Today was Tuesday, and Margaret never bought vegetables on Tuesday. If there was any logic to her habit, it had been lost in all the years of marketing, lost along with the reasons for buying her butter unsalted, her rye bread unsliced, and her tea loose, never in bags. She would no sooner break one of those habits than she would have forgotten to make Oscar's breakfast for all those forty-six years they were married. But now there was only breakfast for one and her little rituals and habits became even more important. They made her feel connected, almost as though nothing had changed in the past thirty years since she moved into the neighborhood.

But she didn't move quickly enough. The thin proprietor, Mrs. Lee, came out onto the street and stopped her before she made it past the tomatoes.

"Ninety-eight cents a pound," she offered. "Special price, Mrs. Binton. Take some now before I sell out." She held up the largest tomato Margaret had seen for a long time. "Just came in from New Jersey."

Margaret studied the tomato for a moment while she tried to figure out the best way to leave without hurting Mrs. Lee's feelings. After all it was Tuesday. But then again, the Lees had moved into the tiny storefront stand only a few months earlier and Margaret didn't want them to get the wrong impression of the neighborhood.

"Thank you, Mrs. Lee," Margaret said. "They are quite attractive, but I'm not shopping today. Just out for a stroll." She picked up one of the tomatoes herself. "New Jersey, you say. So early? Must be hothouse." She smiled politely and thought, Change the subject. "Did you read about the diamond robbery this week, Mrs. Lee? That poor Mrs. Rosenblatt." Carefully she put the tomato back on the pile. The movement did not go unnoticed. Mrs. Lee's face quickly registered her disappointment.

"No, no time to read the paper. Much too busy trying to sell the vegetables. You're sure . . ."

Margaret held up her hand. "I'll be back tomorrow, I promise." She nodded and turned uptown. There, she thought, I don't suppose I've wounded her a bit.

She continued north on Broadway, a favorite among her

many routes since it brought her past many of her old friends. She waved at Sid and Roosa sitting at their bench at Ninety-fourth Street, reading the racing form. Best not to disturb them, she thought. Not while they're trying to figure out the double. Then she spotted Rose sifting through one of the garbage cans on Ninety-seventh. Of course, she thought, Oscar would never have understood her new friendships. She chuckled to herself. But then Oscar was always as conservative as brussels sprouts!

A car screamed around a corner and the noise startled her. She raised a fist in the air and shook it in the direction of the offending vehicle. "Crazy driver," she shouted. But the annoyance gave her an excuse for a cigarette. In one easy, practiced motion she lit a match, held it to a cigarette, then tossed it into the gutter. "Not safe at all in this city," she murmured, then took a puff, stepped off the curb, and continued on her walk. At 102nd Street she turned west toward Riverside Park.

Margaret had good eyes for a woman of seventy-two. She needed glasses only for reading—usually the crosswords— and if anything was a little farsighted. She spotted the fence a good fifty yards away. Now, isn't that interesting, she thought, and crossed the street to get a better look. It was a rough, cheap, chicken-wire fence placed between sections of two-by-fours. The whole unsteady affair ran for about forty feet and closed off an empty lot behind it. On either side were the rough walls of the adjoining tenements. Margaret stopped in front to get a better look. The fence hadn't been there on her last walk.

Margaret was one of those older people who had a peculiar ambivalence about change. She stood in front of the fence for a good five minutes, wondering what had been there and what was coming now. The second thought won out as she watched an old man and three youths picking up bricks, raking glass, and burning trash. But they were at the back of the lot and Margaret felt too shy to call out to them. Instead she studied the section closest to her and was surprised to see the amount of work that had already been done. In the place of rubble she saw a flat, clean patch of maroonish-brown city dirt. Margaret shrugged her shoulders, gave the old man one last glance, then moved away. Another parking lot, she thought. Who needs it!

But in the days ahead as Margaret continued to walk past the empty space, the expected parking lot never materialized. No sign went up, no Tarmac was poured, and no pathetic little shack for the attendant was erected. Just the old man bending and cleaning up, and every now and then some young helpers. The chicken-wire fence was reinforced by cross braces and Margaret finally suspected that what was happening had little to do with capitalism and certainly nothing to do with cars. The only opening in the fence was a small door two feet wide usually padlocked on the inside.

She altered her routine, taking a stroll by the lot every day to check on the progress. Then she began noticing little details. One week it was the stakes in the ground, dividing the area into a checkerboard pattern. The next it was the row of bricks under the strings now attached to the stakes. When shallow trenches appeared, bordering the bricks, and a new, more exciting possibility entered her head, she had to find out.

The old man was near the fence with a shovel, laboring away at a particularly stubborn rock a few inches below the surface. He used the shovel as though he had been born clutching it, or at the very least had invented it. In a minute the rock was dislodged. He turned around and she noticed that his wiry body did not match the lined and worn face. On the other hand, the little fringe of gray hair was just perfect for it. One complemented the other. Margaret got a good look at it as he took off his stained blue baseball cap with the

Yankee logo on it and wiped the top of his head with a red bandanna. He looked up and their eyes met.

"Hot out ain't it?" He smiled. The lines in his face seemed to jump into place, as though they had been put there to respond only to that one expression. Friendly lines, the lines of an old family doctor.

She nodded. "Would you mind," she began, "telling me what you're doing. I've been watching the last few weeks." She pointed. "Is this going to be . . ." She hesitated.

"A garden." He replaced his cap and leaned on the shovel. In that position Margaret thought he looked like an aging Spencer Tracy, except Spencer Tracy wasn't Puerto Rican and this man was.

"A garden?" she repeated. "That's what I thought. But . . ."

The man took a step closer to the fence and gestured behind him. "This, all this, gonna be green. You see, maybe six weeks. Big plants, vines, flowers." His smile broadened and Margaret felt herself smiling with him. The idea alone was a happy one.

"A garden? Here on 102nd Street."

"Specially here on 102nd. Only empty lot I see with good sun." He looked up and for the first time Margaret noticed the entire lot was in sunlight. The tallest building nearby was a five-story brownstone.

"Oh," she said. "And what will you grow?"

"What won't we grow," he answered, and began checking them off on his dirty fingers. "Cucumbers, tomatoes, lettuce, squash, maybe a little eggplant." He stopped for a breath. "Iris, roses, climbing ivy, peas, beans . . ." Margaret held up her hand and he paused.

"You won't forget the marigolds then?" she said. "I mean, if you're doing all those vegetables."

He gave her a look like a prosecuting attorney during a cross-examination.

"What you know about marigolds?" he said.

"What everyone knows who's ever planted a serious garden. They keep away the bugs." He looked at her closely through the chicken wire. "And they're good around tomatoes."

"You kept a garden?"

"Oh, my, yes. For many years . . . in the country." She immediately felt guilty about the little exaggeration. It wasn't really the country. Just a large open field next to her in-laws' apartment in Riverdale. But in those days The Bronx was on the way up and Riverdale—well maybe it was the country.

"You want to help?"

His question brought her back. "Help?"

He looked slightly embarrassed, but the smile was still on his face. "I mean, it's a lot of work and all I got is some kids helping. Sometimes they come, sometimes they don't. I could use someone help me plan, someone I don't have to worry about putting the corn up front where it blocks the sun." He leaned the shovel against the fence. "Not hard work. That's all been done. Some planting. Your own little spot maybe. Something, huh? A little garden middle of Manhattan."

She looked at him carefully for about a half minute. It was hard controlling her excitement. How long had it been since she'd planted a seed and watched it grow?

"My name's Margaret," she said finally.

"Good." He walked over to the little door and opened it. "You can call me Luiz."

3

THE next day precisely at eleven Margaret arrived dressed and ready for work. Her gardening clothes were a mixed arrangement of old stained garments she had found in the back of her closet. She still kept them within reach, like fading memories, unable to discard even the most tattered sweater. This was the second time she'd needed those old clothes, and she smiled when she recalled the last occasion. That had been over a year ago and her association with the police was now purely social. She stopped in at the precinct every month to say hello to her old friends Sergeant Schaeffer and Lieutenant Morley, trying out her latest batch of cookies on them, and then maybe a theory or two about a recent crime. Purely social. "Won't they be surprised when I tell them I'm back in the old duds." She chuckled to herself and knocked on the tiny gate. Luiz was only a few steps away, talking to one of the other helpers. He came over immediately.

"Good morning, Margaret." He beamed. "Right on

time." She passed through the gate and he closed it behind her. He was already reaching into his pocket when she turned to face him. His baseball cap was still on his head. "A present," he said. "Your own key. The last person to leave locks up on their way out." He pressed the key into her hand. "We're not always going to keep people out. Only in the beginning when the seedlings are so fragile."

"You mean it won't be private?"

Luiz laughed. "Oh, no. It's for the community. Whoever helps benefits." He looked at the still empty space. The only speck of green was a hardy city weed growing by one of the walls. "But the first year's always the hardest," he continued. "No one wants to risk all that work if they can't be sure it's gonna produce."

Margaret kicked at the crumbly dirt with the toe of her sneaker. "And will it?"

Luiz rubbed his little stubble of beard and grinned.

"Yes, take my word. And then . . . then we really got something. Then I'm gonna invite some of the kids from the local schools to come around. You know there's kids in this city never seen a tomato grow. You believe that? They must think they're made in factories." He shook his head. "No, not private—for the community. Something nice. Already," he said, "people come. But I only want the workers, not the lookers. Here," he took her gently by the arm, "let me introduce you. Today they're all here." He waved and the five other workers came over.

They were as mixed a bunch of teen-agers as Margaret had ever seen. Or maybe all teen-agers looked like that nowadays she thought. There was long hair, short hair, sneakers, cowboy boots, a Day-Glo T-shirt, a Beethoven sweat shirt, mirrored sunglasses, a mustache, and one youth with a heavy radio playing disco. Four boys and one girl.

"This here is our new helper, Mrs. Binton," Luiz began. "She knows plants, so don't no one give her a hard time."

He smiled with the easygoing confidence of one street person talking to another.

"How do you do?" Margaret said carefully to the assembled group. There was a silence. "Please call me Margaret," she said. "Mrs. Binton is too formal when people are working together." She looked at the boy nearest her and smiled.

"Peter Muñoz," he said quickly and turned away toward Luiz. "Why her?" his eyes seemed to say. His clothes looked out of place, almost too good to be used for gardening. The expensive boots were already covered with mud. Margaret frowned slightly.

"I'm John Kee." A thin Oriental boy held out his hand to her. The smile on his face was open and friendly. "Glad you can help. I don't myself know too much about gardening. I'm hoping I can learn."

"You'd just forget it the next day anyway," Muñoz said. "You got a memory like a sieve." John Kee looked hurt.

"Come on!" Luiz raised his voice. "This ain't the time for jiving." He nodded toward the young girl. "That's Cecile."

Margaret saw the girl, about seventeen, move a step closer. She was the color of freshly roasted coffee and had the body of an athlete, lean in the hips and legs and a back as flat as plywood. The Day-Glo T-shirt hung loosely from her shoulders.

"Hello," the girl said matter-of-factly. She stood there inspecting Margaret. There was something about her eyes, something proud and unyielding that made Margaret feel slightly uncomfortable. She held the girl's stare for a few seconds, then turned to the two boys next to her. The first was wearing the Beethoven sweat shirt. He was smaller than the rest, and chubby, but his face held a certain maturity. Margaret thought he looked like a fifteen-year-old stand-up comic. No one moved. The introduction was becoming awkward.

"I like Beethoven too." She pointed to his sweat shirt. It was the best she could manage.

"Oh, this," he said and glanced down at his chest. "I also got a Led Zeppelin and a Kiss. You caught me in a classical mood." He winked and it seemed to break the tension.

"I suppose they're all good for hoeing," she said.

"Actually I have more luck with Beethoven." He held out his hand. "I'm Jeremiah Stein, but my friends call me Jerry. And this is Vinnie, our rocker, the Upper West Side's answer to Sid Vicious." He nodded to a thin boy with short dark hair and mirrored sunglasses. The last youth looked like one of the P.O.W. victims in a World War II movie, the kind to whom some friendly G.I. would give his K rations. His clothes were ripped in spots and held together with safety pins, and his face, the part that was visible, looked vacant. He seemed uninterested in what was going on around him.

"Lower that some, Tortelli." Luiz pointed to the radio hanging from Vincent's shoulder. The boy reached slowly to his side, chose one of the many knobs, and turned the volume down.

"Vinnie's a good worker," Luiz said, "except he lives inside his radio. He plays those stations like Mangione works a horn."

"Yeah," Vinnie replied. "Long's I got my radio." He grinned. Margaret wished she could see his eyes. "Don't have to put up with no lip from no one but the deejay." He gave an indifferent shrug and his hand strayed back to the controls. She could tell he was anxious to raise the volume again.

"Well, I'm glad to meet all of you," she said brightly. "I guess we'll be seeing a lot of each other."

Cecile shrugged. "Maybe, maybe not."

Margaret started to feel impatient. The girl's indifference surprised her.

"Hey, Cecile," Jerry called. "You trying to be Miss Personality? Come on, give her a chance."

The young girl frowned. "I only meant that some of us got other things going."

"Oh?" Margaret asked politely. "What else do you do?"

The girl's eyes narrowed just the slightest as she took a breath. "Don't see how it's any of your business. Besides," she hesitated, "we don't ask questions like that around here."

Margaret looked confused. "Sorry, I didn't mean to pry." There was silence for a moment. Finally it was broken by John Kee.

"Luiz said you knew about gardens. You know anything about Chinese vegetables?" His face had an open honesty to it that came from his round, smiling eyes. "*Bok tsoi,* things like that?"

"I'm afraid not," Margaret said. "But we can read about them."

"Yeah," he added. "And *gai lan*. That's the best broccoli."

"Maybe we should get back to work," Peter Muñoz said abruptly. He ran a hand through his thick black hair. "I suppose we can always use an extra person in the garden. Less work for the rest of us." He looked down at his muddy boots and frowned. "The sooner it's over the better."

"And snow peas," John Kee continued. "That's my favorite." He looked over at Jerry Stein. "Trouble is," he kicked a toe into the ground, "don't know if this soil's good enough."

"Hey," Jerry said. "You see the size of some of those weeds? 'Course it's good enough. We can even make it better if we put down some manure." He laid a hand on Peter's shoulder. "And I know just where to get some . . . over at the Claremont Stables on Eighty-ninth Street."

Peter brushed the hand off. "Yeah, and who's gonna collect it?" he said in a challenging voice.

"I was thinking of you." Jerry smiled innocently.

"Up yours," Peter said abruptly and walked off.

"I'll get it," Cecile said. "We'll need it if we're going to have an organic garden."

"Organic? I don't know." Luiz scratched his stubble. "I already got some insecticide. Could be trouble without it."

Margaret watched as Cecile's back stiffened. Slowly the girl turned and faced Luiz. "You know what that stuff does?" she asked. "Ruins everything. Things taste awful and all those chemicals gets inside your body and screws it up. Ain't no way I'm gonna work on a garden like that." She shifted her glance to Vinnie, who was standing next to Luiz. "How about you, man? You want that stuff messin' up things?"

Vinnie shrugged. "Hey, what do I know? A tomato's a tomato, right?" He beat a little staccato rhythm on the side of his radio in time with the music. "But if you're gettin' so uptight about it, you can have my vote."

"Cecile's right," John Kee added. "We can always wait until we need it." He looked at Luiz. "I'd prefer if we didn't use it just yet too."

"Well." Luiz shook his head slowly. "If that's what you want. Suppose we can always see about it later." He looked closely at Cecile. "But we can sure use that manure."

"I said I'd get it." She turned abruptly and walked away in the direction Peter had gone.

"Don't mind her," John said after a minute in an embarrassed tone. "Sometimes she can be real friendly."

"Yeah," Jerry added. "Like a wet cat."

4

In the following weeks Margaret never missed a day in the garden. Though she kept busy shopping, visiting her friends, and doing volunteer work three days a week at the Flora K. Bliss old age center, there was something compelling about the ragged lot on 102nd Street. When she was at the Bliss Center she couldn't wait to change into her old clothes and walk the five blocks to the garden to start working. In the evenings she even made rough sketches of possible layouts for the space. The ground now was clear and completely weeded and all the kids were anxious to start planting right away. But Luiz insisted on having the soil tested for acidity and then, after the okay came from the laboratory, he held them up still longer while they worked some fertilizer into the ground. They supplemented the few bags of manure Cecile had collected with a commercial organic fertilizer. The bill came to forty-five dollars including several bags of bone meal and Luiz paid it on his own.

"What else I got to spend my money on?" he had asked innocently. "Garden won't grow good without it, so"—he shrugged—"I bought it."

"But we all could have chipped in," Margaret insisted.

"Your work is help enough," he said simply and went back to turning the fertilizer into the soil.

Margaret didn't realize at first how big the space was. She knew it measured forty by one hundred, but planning with four thousand feet and working with four thousand feet are two different things. Even with seven people, it took the better part of three days to hoe down the area. Finally they were ready for planting. The garden looked perfect. It was all fluffed up like a freshly laundered quilt and smelled like a damp forest. It cried out for seed, and Luiz and his six helpers obliged. The early June weather was just right.

Inside a border of marigolds they planted rows of peppers, spinach, squash, corn, tomatoes, turnips, lettuce, and cucumbers. John Kee even got in a row of snow peas. But the garden was not solely for vegetables, and Margaret made sure there were areas left open for beds of other flowers. Against one side wall they planted fifty feet of climbing ivy to hide some ugly brick. They bought iris and peony bulbs and some baby rosebushes and arranged them in circles and pathways.

It was hard work but no one complained. As the days passed, the young people began to accept Margaret and even rely on her knowledge of gardening. She showed them how to make narrow furrows with a hoe handle and told them the correct spacing for the different vegetables. Then she showed them a few special tricks, ones that even Luiz didn't know, like planting sunflowers in the midst of the beans so that later the thick stalks could be used for the bean poles. In all the work there was only one disagreement and that was about the turnips. Peter Muñoz refused to plant them.

"Slave food," he said, grimacing. "Ain't gonna get me to bust my ass to plant that."

"Damn," Cecile said. "You wouldn't know good food if it sat on you. Slave food!" She shook her head. "Turnips is good for you. Lot of vitamin C."

"There she goes again," Jerry said. "Our resident health freak. Hey, Cecile," he called out, "you eat your ten pounds of brown rice today?"

She picked up her hoe menacingly.

"You shut up. What do you know about right eating anyway. Stuffin' yourself with junk food up at that pool hall all day." Peter laughed and Cecile turned on him. "And you ain't no better. Damn! What you know about bustin yo' ass." She pointed at his neat clothes and shined shoes. "You look like some honky little aristocrat 'fraid to get your fingers dirty."

"Easy," Luiz said, and came over quickly. "Let it pass, Cecile. Peter, why don't you put in that row of peppers over there." He moved grudgingly and before too long everything was back to normal.

It took eight days to finish the planting. There were incessant interruptions from sidewalk superintendents curious enough to look, ask questions, and give free advice, but not interested enough to get involved. One day Luiz had to chase a drunk who kept throwing pint bottles over the fence. Except for Luiz and Margaret, not everyone showed up every day. Vinnie missed one afternoon, and the others showed up when they could. Margaret had to remind herself that they too had private lives, lives that had only been hinted at. And she remembered Cecile's comment. But she couldn't resist. One afternoon she asked Luiz about them.

"I think Peter works downtown," he said. "In the garment center." He shrugged. "The others—I don't know. As long as they stay interested I don't care. Keeps them out of trouble, and look what we did in only two months. A whole abandoned lot cleaned out and planted. I don't care what they do as long as they keep coming."

Margaret nodded. "Yes, I guess you're right," she said. "I'd just like to get to know them better."

5

AFTER the planting came the weeding. The work went more slowly. Fortunately, a solid two days of rain soaked their garden just at the right time.

"Now we get healthy plants," Luiz said. "When the seed is happy, so is the fruit."

Margaret laughed. "Where'd you learn all your gardening?" she asked. "Not in New York."

"No." He scratched his white stubble. "In the most beautiful land of all. In Puerto Rico." He sighed. "But that's a long time ago."

"And now?" she pressed. "Luiz, you never told me what you do. Where the money for all of this comes from; all the seeds, and the tools, that locker we keep them in."

He looked surprised. "The money comes from my job." There was a silence. "Also that old locker which I borrowed. I work, you know, at Yankee Stadium—at night—as one of the grounds keepers."

Margaret's eyes shone.

"It sounded nice to me too," Luiz continued. "But all I do on the field is sweep the paper, rake the base path after the fifth inning, and then when it rains push out the heavy tarps. All I do. Nothing much with the ground. I thought there'd be more, but at least I get to smell the grass," he said. "Most of the time I'm cleaning the seats in the stands. It's better than a factory and then I come here and everything is all right. I live alone; where should I spend all that money if not here? It's all what I want now. Makes me very happy. Maybe you understand. Everything else"—he shrugged—"is gone."

"I understand," she said slowly. "Yes, I certainly do." She felt drawn to this friendly Puerto Rican and his openness. Why is it, she thought, we can communicate with so little and the young people need so much. She lit a cigarette, took a puff, and looked at him.

"Luiz, some Tuesday why don't you come and join us. A bunch of friends and I always get together, sometimes at my apartment, sometimes at the center, and enjoy old times. Maybe we could talk some more. You could tell us about Puerto Rico."

Luiz looked surprised, then slightly embarrassed.

"I don't know, Margaret. Especially around strangers."

She thought a minute. "Well then, just you and me. We'll make it a Monday." She hesitated. "It's only a short walk." She put her hand on his arm. "I'd like to hear more about where you're from."

"Sure," he said. "Okay," and with a certain awkwardness he bent down and began looking for weeds to pick.

"Promise?" Margaret asked.

Luiz nodded shyly.

"Promise what?" Margaret heard and turned to see Peter standing behind her.

"Oh, nothing," Margaret said. "We were just talking."

"What about?"

Luiz stood up with a tight little grin on his face. "Hey, _amigo,_" he said, "how come you got to know everything? You worse than the welfare department."

Peter stiffened. "I didn't think you minded."

The old man reached into his back pocket and withdrew a crumpled box of cigarillos. He took his time to light one. "I don't," he said. "But sometimes I do. Don't take it personal."

Peter shifted uneasily. "Hey, you know me," he said. "Pretty boring around here without the chatter. Especially your stories about the stadium."

"Well then." Luiz put an arm around Peter's shoulder and started walking away with him. He gave Margaret a knowing wink as he left. "I ever tell you about the time Clemente shook my hand?" he said as the two of them walked slowly to the rear of the garden. "Yeah, ask Jerry, he was there. . . ." His voice grew indistinct and Margaret turned back to her weeding.

In the weeks that followed Margaret tried her best to get some of her friends interested in the garden.

"Are you kidding?" her friend Sid had asked. "I buy my vegetables at a grocery where there's no bending over."

"Oh, tosh!" Margaret had snorted, and tried some of the others. Sometimes Rose, Margaret's shopping-bag lady friend, stopped by on her rounds to look in. She'd spend ten minutes chatting with Margaret through the fence, then hike up her bags and continue down the block to the next garbage can.

Only Bertie bothered to come inside the garden. Bertie was her closest friend, and like Margaret, a widow. But, Bertie was cautious. A typical afternoon for her meant sitting in the park and talking to the pigeons that she encouraged to congregate at her feet. That's why Margaret was pleased one Saturday to see her sidle slowly up to the gate and knock timidly on the frame.

"Margaret, can I come in?"

"Sure, Bertie." She opened the gate. Bertie stepped inside and looked around cautiously.

"Whatcha doin'?"

"Pulling weeds. You'd be amazed how quickly they grow . . . even here in the city." She unloaded a handful of them into a paper bag she was carrying. "I think I'm going to talk to Luiz about mulching. This is starting to get out of hand." She passed Bertie the bag. "Come on, we can use your help."

Bertie looked skeptically around her. Little green shoots were just beginning to show through the soil. She bent over slowly and plucked one.

"No, no." Margaret laughed. You just picked a carrot."

"Oh." She threw up her hands. "I don't know, Margaret. I don't think this is my cup of tea. I just came by to see if you wanted to go to a movie this afternoon. There's a Hitchcock double feature at the New Yorker, and I remembered how much you liked them."

"What's playing?"

"*Thirty-nine Steps* and *North by Northwest.*" Bertie's eyes shone. "With Cary Grant."

Margaret grinned. "I'll make you a deal," she said. "If you stay and weed for half an hour I'll clean up and go with you. It's getting late anyway."

"Margaret." Bertie looked crestfallen.

"It's only half an hour. Then we can have dinner after the show at Squires."

"What about my back?"

"Do it a world of good. Come on."

A half hour later on the dot Bertie stood up and groaned.

"Thank God," she said. "Never again."

"Just a minute, and I'll lock up."

Fifteen minutes later the two women were on their way into the loge of the movie theater. It had to be the loge, Margaret insisted. She always smoked at Hitchcock thrillers.

6

It took several Mondays for Margaret to get Luiz to live up to his promise. Finally they walked home together late one afternoon. It was one of those July days that gave summer a good name. The city seemed remarkably clean and everyone in the street looked happy. It was a pleasant walk and they rode her elevator up, talking together easily. Luiz had taken off his baseball cap and Margaret saw some wispy strands of gray hair lightly covering a bald spot. The baldness, she thought, made him look younger and more active.

"Here we are," she said, and led him to her apartment. They entered and Margaret immediately went to the stove.

"How do you like your coffee?"

"The Latino way," he said. "Strong enough to chew."

Margaret laughed. "Sit down. I'll only be a minute."

Luiz found the easy chair and looked around. Her apartment was comfortably furnished with overstuffed chairs and dark, worn oriental rugs. He noticed the small feminine touches, the antimacassars on the back of the couch and the silver candlesticks on a side chest.

"You got a nice place here."

"Thank you. It's too bad the kitchen's so small and right off the living room." She popped her head out of the door. "They call it a Pullman kitchen but it's really nothing more than a closet with gas and running water. There's also a tiny bedroom." She brought over the coffeepot and cake platter. She had bought a fresh streusel on their walk back. "It's all I need, and quite comfortable."

"I see you read a lot." He pointed to a full bookcase.

"Oh, those." She chuckled. "They're only detective stories. I like figuring out the plots. The ones that fool me I put on the top shelf and save. The others I donate to the old age center where I work. Most of them are so silly, quite unbelievable, really." She poured him a cup of coffee. "It's just an escape, I guess. Something like the garden is for you." She looked at him quickly, embarrassed at her own presumption. "I'm sorry. Tell me, Luiz, about Puerto Rico."

He took a sip of coffee and settled back into the chair. "So long ago—I was a farmer. We had a place near Luquillo, my father and brother and me. Maybe only fifty acres, but we grew everything we needed and sold enough to get by. Nice work too. Pineapples are a good crop. Only hard during picking time. We had over thirty-five acres of bushes."

"What happened?"

"They came and offered us a fortune for it. At least it seemed like a fortune then. Five hundred dollars an acre, twenty-five thousand." Luiz scratched his ear. "That was back in '47. We had about three hundred dollars in the bank and twenty-five thousand then was a dream. They even told us we could stay on for a few years until they started construction."

"Construction." Margaret frowned.

"A golf course." Luiz shook his head. "Through all those beautiful pineapple bushes . . . a golf course." He drank the rest of his coffee and she refilled his cup. "It was a shame. We stayed and watched them destroy this living thing. You know about pineapples, Margaret, how they grow? It's like a dance. There's this field and it keeps changing, moving. A bush dies and another grows in its place a few yards away.

After living with them a while you can feel their rhythm, back and forth, back and forth, and then,"—he snapped his fingers—"gone! Three years later my father had to go into the hospital and most of this fortune, this dream, was spent in medical bills. When he came out we were poor again. What little money was left lasted a few years. Then my brother took a job in one of the hotels as a waiter, but I couldn't do that. I couldn't work for them." He paused for a moment. "So I came here. My father died a year after I left. I never saw him again."

"And your brother?"

Liuz shrugged. "Last I heard he was tending bar in San Juan. Who's to say who did right. I never got anything in New York I wanted. Don't think he ever got anything in Puerto Rico either. Just a damn shame about the golf course." He sighed and looked around again. "This is real nice here."

"Thank you." Margaret looked at him. "I'm sorry, Luiz. I can understand how you must feel."

"But that's past. Don't know why I talk about it." He brightened. "There's our garden to think about." He reached out and cut a thin slice of cake. "Coming along pretty nice now, ain't it?"

"How could it otherwise with such a professional in charge. Please, have some more cake."

"Maybe. Only a little piece," he said. "Don't want to spoil my appetite."

"It's only five thirty."

"That's all?" Luiz said. "Okay, maybe a bigger piece. Now"—he looked up—"tell me about you."

"Me?" She lit a cigarette. "What's to tell?"

"There must be something."

An hour later she finally said good-bye to him at the door. Under his arm were two of the mystery books he had asked to borrow and an extra piece of cake she insisted he take. She waved to him as he walked to the elevator.

Such a nice man, she thought and closed the door softly behind him.

7

ONE week later Luiz told her about the cucumber patch. It was a Monday evening, the day before Bertie's birthday. The garden already had a full green growth covering it. The corn was almost a foot high and the squash and cucumber plants had started unfurling their big prickly leaves. Cecile and Vinnie were working in silence by the turnips. John Kee was watering the row of snow peas. The thin hose he was using snaked alongside the wall and was connected to the fire hydrant by the curb. The other two helpers were thinning out plants in the rows of corn. Occasionally Jerry's high-pitched laugh could be heard, probably in response to one of his own jokes. Muñoz stopped every now and then to comb his hair. It was a typical work afternoon. Luiz came over. He looked troubled.

"Have you noticed the cucumbers?" he asked. "Something funny."

"They look fine to me," she said.

Luiz shook his head. "What come up so far is good. But

we planted another hill of seeds and nothing happened there." He walked her over, knelt down, and pointed. Margaret noticed an empty space in the line of cucumbers. "Same seeds," Luiz continued. "We mixed the earth . . . same earth. What could it be?" He lowered his voice. "And look at the squash plants in the next line. What's that cucumber plant doing there?"

Margaret shrugged. "I didn't even notice that."

Luiz stood and looked closer. "It didn't walk."

"No. I'm sure it didn't." Margaret laughed.

"Got to be vandalism. What else. Someone messing around with our seeds. Maybe next the tomatoes. I'm going to check, later when no one's around."

Margaret looked amused. "Luiz, out of all the things we planted one cucumber doesn't germinate in the right place and you see an evil plot. Come on! Everyone knows some seeds just don't take. Besides, I don't believe anyone would do that; certainly none of us." Margaret nodded to the others who were working in the garden. "I think it's wonderful that we're as successful as we are."

"Maybe you're right." He shrugged.

Margaret headed for the gate. "Oh, I'll be here later than usual tomorrow—around four. We're having a little party for a friend. Maybe you'd like to come?"

"No, I'll be here." He cast another glance over his shoulder at the cucumbers. "I hope I'm wrong," he said.

"I'm sure you are."

8

BERTIE's little birthday party was a big success. She spent all morning shopping and by noon everything was ready. The guests started arriving as Bertie was putting the finishing touches to her table. She fluttered about, making sure there were just the right number of plastic spoons and paper doilies.

"Relax," Margaret said. "Everything looks lovely."

"I feel so nervous."

"They're all your friends," Margaret reassured her, and sure enough, within fifteen minutes the room was filled with Bertie's chums from the park. Sid came first, dressed in a gay checkered sport coat and wearing a new paisley bow tie.

"Very distinguished," Margaret said, ushering him in.

"Yes?" Sid smiled. "That's what my bookie said."

Then came old Pancher, grinning from ear to ear. He was carrying the biggest bouquet of flowers Bertie had ever seen.

"Where'd you get those?" she asked.

He looked a little sheepish. "A friend at Riverside

Chapel," he said. "But the funeral was only yesterday so they should be real fresh."

Rena Bernstein came in with a salami from Zabar's. Everyone was in a festive mood. Rose was the last to enter and bustled immediately to the table with the sandwiches. She only paused long enough to drop her shopping bags carefully in a corner.

The wine was the biggest hit. By four o'clock they had gone through the two gallons and Bertie was thinking of sending out for a third. Laughter and cheer filled her small apartment and she was beaming.

"Do you think we need more wine?" she asked Margaret. "We're almost out."

"It won't matter how much you buy. Whenever you invite Roosa you'll always run out." Margaret shook her head ruefully at the small man in the frayed sweater just filling up another glass of wine. "What time is it anyway?" She looked at her watch and started. "Four thirty. Oh, my. I told Luiz I'd see him at four." She leaned and kissed Bertie on the cheek. "Happy birthday, dear. It was a wonderful party. I'm afraid I must go."

"But Margaret . . ."

"No, I really am late. Say good-bye to everyone for me." She turned and made her way out the door.

The only person in the garden when she arrived was John Kee working over his line of snow peas. That's strange, she thought and walked over to where the boy was weeding.

"Hello, Margaret," he said, looking up. "You working today?"

"I came to see Luiz," she said softly. "Did he go?"

"He never came. Least not while I've been here."

Margaret looked around slowly. "When did you get here?"

"One o'clock."

"One!" She frowned. "Did anyone else come?"

"Jerry was in for a while. He just left fifteen minutes ago."

"And you're sure Luiz never showed up?"

"Sure I'm sure." Margaret shook her head slowly and turned to go. John called her back.

"Hey, Margaret, I got a book from the library about growing Chinese vegetables. You want to read it?"

"Some other time," she said. "Not now."

On her way out she glanced at the cucumber patch. It looked as it had the day before.

9

LUIZ did not show up the next two days either. The only thing Margaret could figure was that he was sick. But something kept nagging at the back of her mind, something about their last conversation and his anxiety about the cucumbers. It worried her, and on the third day she decided to do something. But what? She didn't even know his last name. And she had no address . . . just something vague about Harlem, nearby where he worked. That was it! She smiled to herself. They'd know. Maybe they had him working days now. At least they would have an address. She put on a hat and a sweater and walked to the subway. It had been so long since she'd been there that she had to ask the token attendant.

"Excuse me." She smiled politely. "Could you please tell me the quickest way to Yankee Stadium."

Just my luck, she thought angrily. Four stops away from her destination she realized there was a game about to begin. The subway car was packed and people kept trampling on her toes and bumping into her knees. She was relieved when the doors finally opened at 161st Street and River Avenue and the car emptied. She followed the crowd down the steps of the elevated station and stood facing a gleaming Yankee Stadium. All around her she caught snatches of excited conversation. Talk of ERA's and RBI's and names she couldn't understand and had never heard. Joe DiMaggio, she thought, reaching back in her memory for a recognizable name. With that reassurance she moved across the street and waited in the nearest line. In ten minutes she was at the window.

"Upper deck or bleachers?" the man asked.

Margaret blushed. "No, you don't understand. I don't want to get in to see the game, I'm looking for a friend."

The man looked up. "What's that? Upper deck."

"No." Margaret frowned. "He works here."

"Listen, lady, I don't know what you're talking about. This is the ticket line. Game starts in ten minutes."

"How do I get in to see Luiz?"

The man shrugged. "Step aside if you don't want a ticket. Who's next?"

"Okay," Margaret said and shook her head. She reached into her big handbag and pulled out a quarter. "One for the bleachers," she said and gave the ticket seller her angriest look.

"Dollar fifty, lady"

"Of all the nerve . . ." She passed over the extra money and moved with the crowd into the stadium.

Now what? The bleachers were off to the left but she went straight, looking for a door that said EMPLOYEES ONLY. She found herself entering the section of seats directly behind home plate. At first she was amazed at how green the field was as it opened before her. Luminous, she thought, and velvety. A great roar went up and she noticed some men in uniform coming out onto the field. The P.A. system was just introducing "The New York Yankees."

"Ticket please." Margaret looked to her right and there stood a short, wrinkled man in uniform. "Ticket?" he repeated. Margaret almost held out the stub of paper in her hand. Instead she smiled politely.

"No, I'm not here for a seat," she said. "Perhaps you could help, though. I'm looking for a friend who works on the field." She pointed. "Down there. How do I get down there?"

The man frowned.

"What can I do? I've got this important message." The usher looked at her closely.

"Lady, I've been hustled a million times, but I've got to give you credit. That's real smooth." He paused. "What d'ya want? Front-row seat? Cost you twenty."

Margaret laughed. "No, no seat. Really. Just to talk to one of the grounds keepers."

The man was silent for a minute, then shrugged and pointed. "Sorry, lady. Just forget I said anything. Back out that way and turn left. Down a flight to the basement where you see the white door. Comes out into a little lobby, like. Ask someone there." He turned to a person holding out a ticket. "But don't tell 'em it was me gave you the information. Not supposed to let people down during the game."

"Thanks," Margaret said and walked in the direction he had indicated. When she emerged on the floor below, the large carpeted corridor was empty. She walked slowly, studying the different doors that led off in the direction of the field. One said DUGOUT. The one next to that said GROUNDS AND MAINTENANCE. This must be it, she thought, and slowly, hesitantly opened the door.

The room was small, just large enough for a table and a few chairs. It was obvious that this was not an office, but a waiting room for the convenience of employees. Several rakes were propped up in a corner. Three men lounged in the chairs and two were playing checkers at the table a few steps away. Through an open door on the other side of the room she again glimpsed the same luminous green of the playing field.

"Excuse me," she began, and five heads turned in her direction. "I'm looking for Luiz." Two men went back to their checkerboard, but one of the other three came over.

"Valdez?" he asked.

"I guess. Wiry, balding, maybe in his sixties."

"Yeah, that's him. Not here now. He's on nights."

"Has he been here? I mean in the last few days?"

"Come to think of it, no. Was a game two nights ago and I had to fill in for him." The man scratched his chin. "Surprising too. He usually never misses a night. Think he was out the game before that too. That was the Boston one. Five to three. Shame too. All tied going into the ninth." He turned to one of the other men behind him. "Sammy, di'n'tchya fill in on Boston for Valdez?" The man nodded.

"Yeah, Friday night. An' a bitch too. We had to roll out the rugs." Just then a shout exploded into the little room from the open door. "Base hit."

The man turned back to Margaret. "Probably Brown. Whenever he hits right-handed he can belt them all day into the opposite field." He shook his head. "Don't know why they ever switch-hit him left-handed. He has trouble with his stance that side of the plate. Is Valdez sick?"

"I don't know." She thought for a minute. "Where can I get his address?"

"Front office's your best bet." He wrinkled his forehead. "Wait, maybe I got it here." The man turned and opened a small closet. He took out a thin notebook and blew off the light coating of dust on it. "Was a pool on the '78 series. I think all the fellas took a ticket." He looked down the list. "Yeah, here it is. Luiz Valdez." He smiled. "Had New York for the eighth inning of the sixth game, the one Jackson hit his four-hundred-and-fifty-foot homer in. Lucky."

"And an address?"

"Yeah—782 West 128th Street." Margaret copied it down. "Thank you," she said. "You've been very helpful." She took one last look out onto the field, then walked as fast as she could toward the exit.

10

THE address was not hard to find. Number 782 was one of the few lived-in tenements on a block that had more sheet metal covering the windows than glass. The front stoop had a few chips in the concrete and the railings were rusted, but fortunately the names of the tenants had been listed on a cardboard sign. There was an old intercom but it no longer worked. Ripped-out wires protruded from around its edges like some strange electronic growth. Valdez was listed as 4C.

She pushed gently at the foyer door and entered the battered stairwell. She pulled her handbag closer to her side and started to climb. Noises greeted her as she passed the different open doorways on her way; children crying, television sets, sounds of arguing. As she approached the fourth floor, she began to feel an anxiety grip her. She rested on the landing and caught her breath, but the delay didn't help. By the time she found the doorway to 4C with its little tin marker, her heart was pounding faster than ever. She knocked, hesitantly at first, then louder when she got no response.

"Ain't nobody dere," she heard. The voice came from behind her to the left. She turned and found herself looking into the lined face of an old, fragile black woman. She seemed to be suspended in the middle of the doorway where she was standing. Her dress was faded and stained like the walls of the hallway.

"He ain't come or gwan now the pass few days. Ain't borrowed nothin' neither. Mussa leff town."

"No," Margaret said. "He wouldn't do that. Not without telling us."

The black woman studied her silently. Her stare made Margaret even more uncomfortable. Instinctively her hand went for the doorknob.

"Less he's daid," the old woman said casually.

The door opened under her touch and surprised Margaret. She lost her balance for an instant and only recovered by taking a step into the tiny room. The black woman stayed where she was.

The first thing Margaret noticed was the smell. It was not overpowering, just out of place . . . not the kind of thing you'd expect in an apartment. It was metallic and set her teeth on edge. She walked quickly to the stove and turned off the gas. She noticed that the bottom of the aluminum pot was burned almost completely away. Whatever the contents had been was now just a lump of black ashes in the drip pan surrounding the burner. Out of the corner of her eye she saw an explosion of green stains over the sink. She took a step over and touched one of them. It was still liquid and oily, and the pattern on the wall looked like it had been sprayed there. Then she saw the open bottle on the drainboard— Thunderbird wine. It was still half full and contained the same liquid—dishwashing solution. Margaret turned and finally saw the condition of the room. Nothing was in its right place. Chairs were overturned, dresser drawers emptied onto the floor, and clothes strewn about in frantic disorder. Someone had ransacked the room and done a thorough job. Even the few religious pictures had been taken off the wall and the frames smashed in what looked like an attempt to find a cache of money. The mattress was ripped open and the stuffing leaked onto the floor. But no Luiz. Then she saw the closet door and an alarm went off inside her. But it took another minute before she was able to summon her courage and pull the door open.

Luiz lay crumpled in a corner of the tiny closet surrounded by old bundled newspapers and muddy boots. His eyes were open and sightless, a final confusion marked his features. An ugly red welt scarred his forehead and dried blood covered his cheek. But what had killed him was the screwdriver sticking out of his chest . . . right over the heart. Margaret screamed and managed to steady herself on the doorframe.

"He daid then?" the black woman asked. She had crept a few steps into the room.

Margaret nodded and turned away.

"Suppose you'll be wantin' the poleese. Phone's downstairs."

Margaret started to go.

"Pay phone. Cost you a dime," and she followed Margaret out of the room as silently as she had entered it.

11

MARGARET waited until ten o'clock that night before leaving her apartment. She was exhausted after all the commotion and the two-hour delay with the police. The shock of Luiz's murder was just beginning to wear off, and in its place an anger was growing. She had felt its first stirrings in the tiny apartment, listening to the strange policeman run through his standard interrogation, hearing the negative, listless replies of the black woman: "No, suh, didn't hear nuthin'—see nuthin' neither." The anger deepened when she realized that no one really cared. Other people in the building shrugged as though it were a normal part of life to have a neighbor murdered. Then she saw the reality. If something were to be done, she'd have to do it herself.

Margaret knocked softly on the door and waited. In a minute Bertie appeared.

"Are you ready?"

Her friend started fidgeting with the doorknob.

"I don't know, Margaret. It's so late."

"You promised on the phone, Bertie." Margaret looked cross. "I told you I need you to hold the flashlight."

"But, Margaret . . ."

"Come on, we'll be back by eleven." Bertie heaved a sigh and opened the door wider.

"Okay, but only for you, Margaret. I'll just be a minute."

There was enough light filtering down the block from the streetlamp for Margaret to see the keyhole in the padlock. The little door made only the slightest creak as she undid the hasp and opened it. Together the two women crept into the dark garden and over to the thin metal locker that was the toolbox. Bertie had her hand on Margaret's shoulder and walked with short, halting steps. She was mumbling to herself.

"Shhh," Margaret cautioned and slowly lifted out a shovel.

"This is crazy," Bertie hissed. "We'll be caught."

"Nonsense. Follow me and keep the light low to the ground."

Margaret found the cucumber line and walked to the open space. She dug the shovel into the earth and made a small hole, delicately putting the removed dirt into a separate pile.

"Must be careful. It can't look any different tomorrow." She took another shovelful and straightened up. Her hand was at her back.

"What's the matter?" Bertie turned off the flashlight.

"Nothing. I can't go as quickly as I thought." Bertie hesitated for a second.

"Maybe we should take turns."

Margaret's smile was lost in the darkness. "That's sweet of you, Bertie." She gripped the shovel again and took another scoop. "Ten minutes on, ten minutes off."

For the next forty-five minutes the two women worked on the enlarging hole. Margaret suggested they dig down two feet, then widen it. So far they had gotten only exhausted and dirty from their efforts. They kept their voices to a whisper and the noise of traffic masked the sound of the shovel. They were nearing the other cucumber plants when Bertie straightened up and shook her head.

"Whatever you're looking for, it isn't here."

"It's got to be. We have to go deeper."

"Deeper!" Bertie let out a groan. "My legs are killing me."

"Another foot," Margaret said, and took the shovel. She walked over to the middle of the hole and sunk it in. Both women heard the metallic sound it made as it hit something solid.

"Quick, the light." Margaret found the edge of the object and started digging around it. Bertie huddled closer and watched as a metal box began to emerge.

"Brand new," she said. "Fancy that."

"I think I can get it now." Margaret laid the shovel down and reached into the hole. When she straightened up, she was holding a small index-card file.

"Is it heavy?"

"There's something inside, but it's locked. Maybe I have something at home." She looked around her. "Let's put all the dirt back. I'll rake it over to blend it in."

In fifteen minutes the hole was filled and well camouflaged. Margaret picked up the metal box and followed Bertie to the gate. It was not until they had reset the padlock and walked a dozen yards away that Bertie was able to speak.

"*Gawd*. My heart's still pounding. What do you suppose is in there?"

"Don't know," Margaret said. "But it sure meant a lot to someone."

Twenty minutes later the metal box sat in the middle of Margaret's dining-room table. The only other objects on the surface were two steaming cups of tea and a plate of biscuits. Margaret found her longest sewing needle and came back to the table.

"Let's see if this will do. I once saw an old film where they opened a lock with a needle." She pushed it in and started twisting. "But they never tell you exactly what to do with it. It all looks so easy."

Bertie's eyes were on Margaret's hands.

"Maybe you should get a hammer."

"Then what?"

"I don't know. Bash it open."

"Bertie!" Margaret shook her head slowly. She gave the needle a particularly sharp turn. "Ouch!" Her hand jerked away. "This needle's too thin." She pulled it out and put it back in the sewing kit.

"How about a bobby pin?"

"No, I'll try this." Margaret reached up and withdrew the long hatpin she wore through the bun on her head. "This thing's got a thousand uses. Maybe this is one of them." She took another sip of tea, stuffed a biscuit into her mouth, and started working with the hatpin.

"Maybe a locksmith . . ." Bertie began.

"I think I'm getting something." She felt a little click, and the pin slipped an eighth of an inch deeper into the lock. She levered it to the left, then right, and suddenly the top un-seated as the lock released.

"There," Margaret said and sat back. Bertie's mouth was open.

"I never knew you could do that."

"Neither did I." She replaced the pin in her hair and pulled the box closer. "Now let's see what this is all about." She lifted up the top and both women stared down at a fortune in cut diamonds.

12

LIEUTENANT Morley leaned back in the swivel chair and lit a cigarette. His uniform shirt was pulling across his chest and made him look heavier than his 195 pounds. There was a sprinkling of gray in his sideburns and his face had a tired expression. If it hadn't been for his alert blue eyes, he could easily have passed as a retired carpet salesman.

Sergeant Schaeffer lounged in a seat nearby. He looked more like a tapped-out, street-worn junkie than the thirty-four-year-old crack policeman he was. His full beard hid a strong chin and the one-inch scar where a gunman's bullet had almost blown his jaw away. The little gold earring in his left ear was a recent addition and did much to complement his stained, tie-dyed undershirt. He had stretched his sandaled feet out on top of a typing desk, making himself look longer than his six foot one inch height. His eyes were on his boss.

"It's out of our district," Morley said. "Sorry, Margaret, there's nothing I can do. The man was killed in the Twenty-sixth and they'll have to handle it. Gondolpho's good. Don't worry.'' He looked slowly to his right to see Schaeffer's reaction. Schaeffer played with a small hole in his blue jeans for a minute, then turned toward Margaret. She was sitting across the desk from Morley.

''Margaret,'' Schaeffer began reluctantly, ''I understand how you feel. But we've got our hands full.''

''Yeah,'' Morley said, swinging back upright. ''And enough of our own cases without importing them. Besides, you shouldn't get involved. Let the police handle it.''

Margaret cleared her throat and reached for one of Morley's Camels. She looked silently from one to the other as she lit it, then tossed the match into the crowded ashtray.

''Now you listen to me, Lieutenant Morley. And you too, David. I've been coming here giving you advice for the last year. Luiz was my friend and now I need help. I'm not going to sit by and watch a bunch of strangers go through some official motions and then take the easy way out. I know how they handle those things.'' She took a puff on the cigarette. ''Poor and Puerto Rican. If they spend two days on it, that's a lot. Already the investigating officer was talking about maybe some junkie doing it. See, he was falling for the ruse and I didn't like it at all.'' She leaned forward and sent an ash into the ashtray. ''That's why I didn't tell him a thing.''

Morley raised an eyebrow.

'' 'Cept of course the obvious—that we were friends.''

''There's more?'' Morley asked.

''Sure there's more, but I wasn't going to tell him. I had to do a little investigating first. Last night.''

''I don't follow you,'' Schaeffer began. ''The murder is still in the Twenty-sixth.''

''But *this,* '' she said and pulled out the gray file box, ''is in the Eighty-first.'' She stood up and placed it in front of the lieutenant. Morley frowned, then opened the lid slowly.

Schaeffer watched his expression change. The look Morley gave Margaret could have fried an egg.

"Where'd you get these?"

"In your precinct," she said politely. "Now are you interested?"

"What is it, Sam?" Schaeffer got up and took a step closer.

Morley hesitated. "I think it's the Rosenblatt job," he said. He reached out and lit another cigarette. "Yes, damn it, I am interested."

"I thought you'd be." Margaret smiled. "Now here's what's happened."

It took only ten minutes for her to tell the story. She talked about Luiz's suspicions and her finding the stones in the cucumber line with Bertie. Then she described the disarray at the scene of the murder. "An obvious faked robbery," she concluded. "Although the flunkies up in the Twenty-sixth won't believe it. No, it's up to us now. If we leave it to them we'll never find the murderer. There's an obvious connection. Catch the Rosenblatt thief and you'll get Luiz's killer, although, to tell the truth, I'm not sure I understand what those stones were ever doing in our cucumber line."

Morley picked out one of the diamonds and held it to the light. A dozen pinpricks of color danced on the wall behind him as he moved the stone between his fingers. "That's simple," Morley said as he replaced it in the box. "This stuff's so hot right now it's almost impossible to fence—would need an international organization and even then it wouldn't be safe. The insurance company and Interpol have tracers out all over the world. Locally there's a whole army of informers just dying to free-lance the thing. Even the smallest lead and we'd hear about it. So far, as I understand it, there's nothing. Can mean only one thing."

"And what is that?" Margaret asked.

"A local job by a small-timer. Maybe he was figuring on a few grand he could hock with a neighborhood fence. All of a sudden he's got a quarter of a million dollars of hot ice and nowhere to go with it. So he does the only sensible thing—he buries it in the hope things will blow over. Six months, maybe a year. The pressure would be off and he could start dealing them." Morley ran a thick hand through the sparse covering of hair on his head. "Enter your little garden and the perfect crib for the loot. That's what they were doing in the cucumbers, Margaret, and it might have worked if your friend Luiz hadn't been so suspicious." He turned toward Schaeffer. "What do you think?"

Schaeffer rubbed his forearm, then looked up.

"I think Margaret's brought us another one, Sam."

"Yeah, but how do we handle it? Gondolpho's already started his investigation. We bring him in? Hand him this info? What?" The two policemen were silent for a moment.

"Can't we wait," Margaret asked, "until we catch the murderer ourselves?"

Schaeffer chuckled. Morley just scowled. "How? You got any bright ideas?"

"That's easy," she said. "First we put the diamonds back."

"What!" Both men said it at once.

"Rebury the diamonds. It's no good catching the thief without the loot. Nab him when he's digging them up, or when he's leaving the garden with them."

"And how do you propose to know when he'll move?" Morley said skeptically. "Send him an invitation?"

"Force his hand."

"How?"

"Close the garden. You're the cops, ain'tcha?"

The two policemen looked at each other. A grin was just beginning to show on the corners of Schaeffer's mouth.

"Could we do that?" he asked. "Just tack up a notice and close it?"

"Yeah. We can find some excuse," Morley said. "We'll catch some heat from the community, but we can do it." He got up and walked the two steps to the window. When he came back, his face was creased with worry. "I just hate like hell sticking a quarter of a million bucks back in the ground."

"Margaret's right, Sam. We got to catch him loaded. If we can pin the robbery, we should get a murder one, too." He turned back to Margaret. "Who else has access to that garden?"

"It's just those five kids I told you about—unless they're careless with their keys."

"A padlock?" Schaeffer asked.

Margaret nodded. "Here." She reached in and pulled out her key. The sergeant studied it for a minute.

"Damn. You could pick it with a toothbrush."

"Have you noticed anyone suspicious?" Morley interjected. "Snooping around the garden, maybe waiting for everyone to leave?"

Margaret shook her head. "People from the community are always stopping by to look in. Everyone's curious about the garden, but no one in particular." She thought for a minute. "No, no one I'd call suspicious."

Morley sat back down heavily. "What kind of stake could we do? Any problems?"

"Don't think so," Schaeffer answered. "I've walked by there a few times. Looks pretty clean. No alleys or exits except the one in front. A clear view from across the street. We've got the equipment. You can put Jacobson on the hot dog wagon during the day just in case, and I can work the TV repair van at night. Anyone setting foot in that garden will be spotted right away. I think we could risk it."

Morley was silent, looking down at the diamonds. He

jiggled the box back and forth and watched as the light refracted off the stones and came back at him in a shower of colors. He took a deep breath.

"If we lose them, it's my neck."

"Sam, it's our only handle. If you turn them in, we might as well kiss Valdez's killer good-bye. Gondolpho may be good, but Margaret's right. To them it's strictly a bottom priority case. I think we owe her a shot."

"Okay, okay. Tell Jacobson." Morley stabbed his cigarette out, closed the box, and carefully slid it across the desk to Schaeffer. "Check it out for prints, then put it back tonight. We'll close the garden tomorrow. Take Margaret with you to show you where it goes."

Margaret's face beamed. "Oh, yes, one last thing," she asked. "What about Bertie? She's so curious, you know. She was with me."

"Can you trust her?" Morley looked displeased.

"I think so."

"Okay, but no one else. I don't want to blow the operation because some old lady gossips to the wrong person." Immediately after he said it he felt embarrassed. "I'm sorry, Margaret. You know what I mean. We got to be careful."

"Oh, Bertie doesn't gossip," Margaret said, getting up. "Except to her pigeons. She'll understand."

"Good. Let's hope this works."

"If it doesn't," she said, turning toward the door, "I'll be very surprised."

13

WHEN Margaret arrived the following afternoon, there was already a small commotion outside the little garden. A policeman she had never seen was standing near the front of the gate. All five of the helpers were shouting and pacing back and forth on the pavement, and a little group of onlookers had formed. John Kee spotted her first and ran anxiously over.

"They're going to lock us out," he shouted. "Can't you do something? He says we don't have the right to be here." He looked on the verge of tears. "Maybe he'll listen to you."

"Lock us out?" Margaret tried to sound surprised. This was going to be a difficult role, playing both sides. "How can they do that?" She pulled her handbag closer and walked boldly toward the policeman.

"You have no right—"

He shook his head. "Sorry, ma'am. Orders. We're closing it up at the end of the week."

"What's this all about?" She glanced around and noticed that the five teen-agers had moved in back of her in a semicircle. Behind them the rest of the onlookers were standing in a tight knot. She'd have to play it out.

"Just doin' what I'm told," the cop said. "You want to find out more, go to the Eighty-first Precinct. . . . Speak to Lieutenant Morley."

There were angry shouts behind her.

"You can't do this," she said, frowning.

"Look, lady. No arguments. I came down to inform you, that's all . . . give you a chance to get your stuff out." He was starting to look uncomfortable. Margaret hesitated for a moment.

"Where is this precinct?" she asked. "After all the work we've done . . ."

He gave her the address. She turned to the group behind her.

"We've got to speak to this Officer Morley. This one doesn't know anything. Come on." She started walking away. Not everyone followed. By the time she marched into the precinct house, there were only nine other people with her, the five helpers and four of the more interested bystanders. Morley came out of his office when he heard the commotion in front of the booking desk.

"What's this?"

Margaret turned to glare at him. For an instant her face softened and she gave him a little helpless look. Then her eyes turned icy again.

"We've come to complain," she began, "about the closing of our garden. Who's Morley?"

The lieutenant had to stifle a grin. "That's me."

"What's the idea?" she continued. "No one's using the place."

"Sorry," he said. "The lot belongs to someone who sent in a complaint." He looked over the rest of the gathering.

"You can't just confiscate property in this city. Besides, you've been using water from fire hydrants, which is dangerous and illegal.''

One of the bystanders pushed her way to the front. She was a woman in her forties, attired in a plain brown cotton dress and Dr. Scholl's shoes. Her hair was done in a tight little efficient cut—nothing excessive.

"That lot's been empty for years," she began. "And what they're doing is the best thing that's happened on that block.''

"It's private property.''

"Private!" The woman pointed a finger at Morley's chest. "If the owners don't use it or maintain it they shouldn't be allowed to keep it. It was always an eyesore." Her face was changing color with excitement. "You'll hear about this. I write for the local paper.''

Morley shrugged. "Suit yourself. All I know is Friday night we lock it up. You can write all you want and it won't do any good." Morley turned to go. A clamor of angry voices followed him as he entered his office. The last thing he heard was Margaret saying, "You'll see!" He closed the door and shook his head.

"A little heat?" Schaeffer asked. He was still sitting in the chair by the desk where Morley had left him.

"We'll be all right. Who owns that property anyway?"

Schaeffer shrugged. "What's it matter? By Friday night it'll be over and you can let them go back.''

"Yeah, I suppose." He sank heavily into his chair and lit a cigarette. "Bury the stuff okay?"

Schaeffer nodded. "Yeah. No prints except Margaret's. Wiped clean.''

"Figures." Morley inhaled and watched as the smoke lifted to the ceiling. He laughed softly to himself. "You know, that Margaret's quite an actress.''

14

SCHAEFFER stayed up all night with both eyes glued to the one-way mirror in the van. He had the walkie-talkie on the seat next to him ready to call in the backup car, but nothing happened. He watched as a hazy dawn illuminated the garden. Within half an hour sounds of traffic started to drift past him. He yawned and looked at his watch. God, how he hated stakeouts! It was 6:45.

Forty-five minutes later Jacobson finally arrived with two containers of coffee.

"Anything?"

Schaeffer shook his head.

"Staunton's bringing the wagon over at nine. I'll take it from you now. Go home. You look like you could use the sleep."

Schaeffer got up and stretched his legs, then moved to the back of the van and opened the door.

"Have fun."

"Morley's expecting you at four thirty."

He eased out of the truck and started walking to his apartment. Maybe it's too soon, he thought. Wait till the word gets out.

A newspaper was open on Morley's desk when Schaeffer entered later that afternoon. It was one of the local, West Side rags, but what it lacked in circulation, it made up for in rhetoric.

" 'Police Kill Garden, Community Incensed.' " Schaeffer picked it up and read down the first column.

"Good coverage," he said. "Should do the trick."

"It better!" Morley looked annoyed. "I don't like seeing my name in print. That bitch really did a number on us. . . . Woulda thought we closed down Central Park."

"Anything from Jacobson?"

"You kidding? He just phoned. They're holding a meeting out front. Thirty, forty people there."

Schaeffer looked amused. "You mean we're going to have a fight on our hands?"

"That's the last thing I want. If this thing escalates it'll set our community relations program back ten years. Dillon was already on my ass for half an hour this morning."

"Did you tell him?"

"I told him to get stuffed. He's still a sergeant." Morley leaned forward and lifted the newspaper. "And this isn't the end of it. One of the dailies might pick it up and then we're really in hot water. Our boy better move soon."

"Probably tonight. What are they meeting about?"

"Who knows? Maybe a lecture on civil disobedience."

"Was Margaret there?"

"Margaret, goddamnit, was doing most of the talking!"

They didn't have long to wait. This time there were too many people to fit into the small front room of the precinct. Morley had to meet them outside on the street. The woman journalist was in the front, waving a group of papers with several signatures. Margaret was staying discreetly on the side.

"I've got over a hundred names," the woman was saying. "There're more coming. Names of people who think this is the most outrageous thing the police have done." She turned behind her to pick up the vocal support of the others. "We want to know who the owner is. We want to meet him face to face." She took a step forward and thrust out the papers. "Here!" Morley reached for them casually.

"Now listen—" He tried to address them all.

"No, you listen!" the woman broke in. "There's been nothing but hostility from the police. You've made no attempt to dissuade this phantom owner from locking us out. Yesterday you stonewalled the issue and turned your back on the whole thing. Why? What's in it for you? Gardens are good for communities. This is shocking!" There was a rumble behind her and Morley knew he was fighting a losing battle.

"My hands are tied" was all he said. "You want to get it open after Friday, speak to the owner."

There were loud shouts now from all sides.

"Who is the owner?" the woman demanded. For a split second Morley looked pained. Margaret caught it and came forward.

"Perhaps this is not the best way," she said, turning to the crowd. "I can see that now. I suggest a committee. Maybe Lieutenant Morley will be good enough to sit down with a few of us and discuss this in private." She faced the journalist. "You can't force the police, at least not this way."

"But, Mrs. Binton." The woman looked surprised. She motioned to Morley. "They don't know from discussions, from reason. All they know is coercion. That's what we're here for. You said so yourself."

"No, what I said is that we should talk with them, show

them our petitions. I didn't say we should attack them. Can't you see you're not getting anywhere your way? They just dig in further.'' She took a step closer to Morley. ''How about it, Lieutenant? Would you be willing to meet with us? Just a small group?''

He picked up on the opportunity. ''Yes.''

There was a grumbling from the onlookers. ''Tomorrow. Today''—he shrugged—''I can't help you.''

''Mrs. Schwartz?'' Margaret looked at the journalist for her approval.

''Already a stall! I don't like it.''

''You don't want to meet with us?'' Margaret asked.

''I'll be there. I'm just not going to sit around and wait, that's all.''

''Thank you.'' Margaret faced the crowd. ''Two or three more. How about you, Jerry, and maybe Mrs. Slawson.'' She pointed to a small, inconspicuous woman in the crowd. They both nodded. ''Then, what time?'' She turned back to Morley.

''Two o'clock.''

''Two it is,'' she said. ''We'll see you then.''

''Really dug you a hole this time,'' Schaeffer said as Morley entered the precinct. ''I heard.''

''It gives us another night. What's Gondolpho up to?''

Schaeffer smirked. ''I got a friend over in the Twenty-sixth. I expressed a little interest in the Valdez case so he drops me a bone once in a while. No prints on the murder weapon. It was a Phillips screwdriver, old. They won't be able to trace it. Stabbed twice in the heart somewhere near the door then dragged into the closet. Again, no prints anywhere. Margaret got it right. They're tagging it a simple robbery. They can't pry a lead from anyone so it's simplest to pigeonhole it that way. Murderer was too careful.''

''Maybe we shoulda been careful too,'' Morley said.

"Given the stones back. Big splash in the dailies. Not this crap we're getting."

"It's too late, Sam. We're in this deep, we can't go back. I just hope something drops tonight."

"You and me both."

15

It was three hours into the stakeout later that night when Schaeffer first noticed the figure lounging in one of the doorways down the block. Schaeffer had that policeman's sixth sense, that ability to feel when something criminal is about to happen. The doorway the man was standing in had been used earlier by others to get out of the light drizzle that was falling. But now there was something strange. Perhaps it was the number of glances the figure gave down the block in the direction of the garden; perhaps it was just the alert way he was standing. But Schaeffer knew something was about to happen. He picked up the walkie-talkie and whispered into it. Then he moved closer to the window and waited.

It took fifteen minutes for the figure to move, but when he did, it was in the right direction, down the block and across from Schaeffer. He stopped right in front of the garden and leaned against the fence. Schaeffer caught a brief look at his face as he lit a cigarette. He tried to remember the details:

knifelike nose, glasses, curly hair. The radio crackled and he heard Staunton's voice.

"I see the guy in front of the garden. You want us to close?"

"Not yet. Let him make his move." He put the radio down softly and continued to watch. But something was nagging at him. A disappointment. He couldn't place it, but something was off. And yet, the son-of-a-bitch was carrying a piece. He could see the slight bulge under the left arm. He warned Staunton. Still nothing. Then footsteps from the right and Schaeffer saw the second man, a big black walking straight as an arrow for the garden. The two men met at the little door and turned their backs, but not completely. Schaeffer spotted the small package change hands, then the money. Then he knew what had been disturbing him: no flashlight. The interior of the garden was pitch black.

"Lay off. We got us a drug deal. I don't want to blow the stake by busting them."

"Just a lousy buy?" Staunton breathed into the walkie-talkie.

"Yeah. See if you can make the dealer if he passes you. The thin one. But no flashing lights on the block."

"Ten four. I'll relay it." There was a silence for a moment. "Too bad. Thought we had something."

"Me too." Schaeffer turned again and saw the two men separate. The transaction was over in less than a minute. Schaeffer had witnessed it dozens of times and it still amazed him how quickly it all went. No haggling, no inspection. Just supply and demand. Only one of the many street transactions that kept the pipeline flowing. He leaned over, grabbed a cigarette from his pack, and lit it slowly. By the time he extinguished the match and looked out the window again, the block was empty. "Shmuck," he mumbled to himself. "I shoulda seen that coming."

*   *   *

It was the only excitement all night. Schaeffer dragged himself into Morley's office at 9:00 A.M. and told him the bad news.

"I guess he figures he can wait us out," Schaeffer said wearily. "With all the pressure from the community he must feel it's still pretty safe. I guarantee you those stones are still there."

"Christ!" Morley stabbed out a cigarette and quickly lit another. He flipped the morning edition of *The New York Times* in front of Schaeffer. "Page two of the second section, the small article on the left. You can bet tomorrow's will be bigger."

Schaeffer read it slowly, then looked up.

"I'm glad it's you pulling the weight and not me."

Morley looked disgusted. "This is really sticking it to me. If it weren't Margaret I'd dig those stones up in a goddamned minute. I don't like playing the heavy."

"Listen, Sam, it was murder," Schaeffer said.

"Not in my precinct!"

Schaeffer got up and moved to the door. "I gotta get some sleep. Good luck this afternoon. Just don't take it out on Margaret."

"That's exactly who should get it."

The phone rang as Schaeffer closed the door. Morley lifted the receiver and answered angrily, "Yeah, what is it?"

His body stiffened when the caller identified himself. He'd already heard that gravelly voice before on TV. It was Horgan, the chief of police.

"I want to see you at two o'clock about this garden bullshit."

"I'm having a meeting at two," Morley said without thinking. "With some of them."

"Postpone the goddamn meeting." The voice sounded annoyed, used to being obeyed. "I want to know what the hell's going on."

"Yes, sir." Morley grimaced. Now came the real heat.

16

MARGARET was on her way out to do her Thursday marketing when Morley called. Lucky for him, she thought. Ten minutes more and I would have been at the A & P. Fortunately she had Mrs. Schwartz's number at the paper. She relayed the information. "Can you call Mrs. Slawson?" Margaret asked. "Tell her about the delay. I'll have to find Jerry. That's right. Four o'clock, not two." She put down the phone and looked appraisingly at her shopping cart. Well, it would have to wait, that's all. She had no idea where to find her young helper and it might take time. She still had a few Stouffers in the freezer. She'd get by on the frozen tuna casserole. She wheeled the cart back into the closet and headed outside.

The chicken-wire fence of the little garden was now covered with hastily lettered signs all complaining about the closing. There were only a few people in front: some of the curious of the block, one or two of the loudest supporters, and Peter Muñoz. Margaret walked over to him and said hello.

"Hey, what's happening!" He flashed Margaret a big smile. She noticed that he was wearing tight-fitting slacks and an acetate shirt. His expensive boots looked freshly polished. The open shirt showed the thick gold chain around his neck. His eyes darted over the few people in the crowd before they came back to Margaret.

"This is something else," he said. "I mean I hear we got a TV crew coming later. You know, like for tonight on the news."

"Really." Margaret tried to sound pleased. "Listen, Peter, I've got to find Jerry. That meeting at two was postponed. You know where he might be?"

"Stein?" Muñoz laughed. "Only one place he would be if he ain't here: at Game City."

"Game City?" Margaret looked confused.

"105th and Broadway. You know, Ping-Pong, chess, pool. He usually goes there to hustle up a few dollars."

"Jerry?"

Muñoz nodded. "I hear he's got the best cut serve north of Ninety-sixth Street. Yeah, he's probably there now."

"105th and Broadway?"

He nodded again.

"As long as you're here," Margaret said, "there's also a few things I wanted to ask you."

The boy looked down at his watch and raised an eyebrow. "Jesus. Ten already." He started to turn away. "Sorry, I told them at the shop I was taking my mother to the doctor's. Gotta get back by break time." He smiled. "I wanted to check out the action over here."

"Where can I talk to you?" she shouted after him.

"C and J Casuals. Thirty-ninth Street and Seventh."

Margaret barely caught the address, he was moving so quickly. She saw him round the corner and head downtown for the subway. She walked slowly behind him, but when she got to Broadway, she turned north.

"Game City," she said softly and shook her head disapprovingly.

The amusement center was located on the second floor of a five-story loft building overlooking Broadway. From where she stood on the pavement, Margaret could only see the players' heads through the big picture windows, moving back and forth in strange disembodied duets. Occasionally someone would lift a hand that held a paddle. It was the reassurance she needed to enter the building. Ping-Pong was a game she had played as a child, a proper game played in millions of homes. It was only when she emerged into the large, noisy game floor that she had a momentary hesitation about continuing. But then she figured, I'm here now, and began searching the crowd for Jerry.

Half the space was taken up by Ping-Pong tables. The other half was divided into pool and chess. Most of the people were evenly spaced, but here and there a small group was gathered near one table, watching a particular match. There was little conversation over the noise of a dozen bouncing balls, hammered tables, and the occasional curse. The room was humid and made Margaret uncomfortable. A cloying, noxious smell came from the overflowing ashtrays. Margaret lit her own cigarette and spotted Jerry playing near the far wall. She walked slowly over, ignoring the several curious stares she got on the way.

The man he was playing was much older, a wiry, mustachioed, David Niven type with rolled-up sleeves. Something about his face told Margaret he was losing.

"14–16," Jerry said. "You serve. Five quick ones and I'm in for another ten. It's pigeons like you that keep me fed."

The man served the ball so fast Margaret had trouble

seeing it. Jerry just managed to get it back and his opponent killed it in the corner. Without hesitation he served it again, and this time Jerry missed it completely. "Sixes," he said. "Damn, that's enough of that." But he lost the next one after a long rally and then put two into the net.

"19–16," the man said with a smirk. "Now who's the pigeon." Jerry was bent slightly over, but now he stood up to his maximum five feet five inches. The crowd was silent.

"Double or nothing?" Jerry said. "Easy bet for you."

"You're on." The thin man flipped the ball over the net and waited.

It wasn't so much the speed of Jerry's serve that Margaret marveled at later, but the funny bounce it took when it landed on the other side of the table. One time it hopped right up and seemed to fly off the opponent's paddle. Another time it sank like it had a lead core. Jerry took all five of his serves and won the game.

"Let's see." He made a quick calculation. "Two at ten and the last at twenty." He held out his hand. "That's forty dollars."

"Damn if I ain't been hustled," the man said angrily, but then reached into his back pocket.

"S'what they all say." Jerry took the money. "Thanks." He turned to pick up his paddle and saw Margaret watching him. His face ran through a series of expressions before he settled on one he felt was appropriate. He approached with a wry smile.

"Caught me," he said. "What are you doin' here?"

She just shook her head. "Where'd you learn that serve?"

"At Boy Scout camp while everyone else was out tying knots." He looked at her closely. "Seriously, Margaret. What's up?"

"The meeting was postponed until four, but I wanted to talk to you. It's a little noisy . . . ."

"The snack bar," he said. "It's through that door." She

followed him and took a seat at one of the small Formica tables. It was a tiny room filled with automatic dispensing machines.

"Want something?"

Margaret looked skeptically at the selections.

"Tea," she said. "This won't take long."

He brought the cup over and sat next to her. He started working on a Hershey bar and his own orange soda.

"What won't take long?"

"Oh, nothing," she said casually. "Jerry, tell me something. How come you're not in school, a bright boy like you?"

"I graduated last year."

"And no college?"

"More money in New York." He fingered the bills in his shirt pocket. "Anyway, I read a lot."

"And your parents let you—"

"My parents are dead," Jerry interrupted. "I live with an older brother and he could care less."

"Oh." Margaret bent over the tea again. "I'm sorry."

"You walk all this way to find out how come I'm not premed at NYU? Margaret, I gotta feel honored." He looked at her closely. "And also a little suspicious."

She smiled thinly. "No, Jerry. I came to ask you about the garden and whether you might . . ." She hesitated for a moment. ". . . might have seen anything strange."

The teen-ager took a swallow of soda and looked straight at her.

"You mean if I know what happened to Luiz."

Margaret's face fell. "What?"

"It is about Luiz, isn't it? I knew something was wrong when he didn't show all week."

Margaret took a big swallow of the tasteless fluid.

"He's dead," she said slowly.

Now Jerry looked surprised. "Dead? A heart attack?" He

glanced down quickly at the chocolate bar for a moment. When he raised his eyes again, he said almost in a whisper, "Killed?"

Margaret nodded. It would have to come out. "It looks like someone killed him, then robbed him." She watched his reaction. Either it was genuine surprise or Jerry was as good an actor as he was a Ping-Pong player.

"Who would do that?" he asked. "Nice old guy like him. All he wanted was to work in the garden."

Margaret waited a minute. "How'd you meet him, Jerry?" The boy's eyes narrowed as though he were remembering something from too long ago.

"I went to The Bronx High School of Science and used to cut classes now and then. Didn't matter, I finished with straight A's anyway. But Yankee Stadium wasn't too far away and I'd go if there was a good game on. If Boston was playing or Catfish was pitching."

"Catfish?"

"Yeah, Hunter." He continued. "Only I used to sneak in. There was this loose railing that only a few of us knew about. One day Luiz caught me."

"What happened?"

"He told me that if he ever caught me again he'd take me to the security guys. Then he brought me with him to the playing field and let me watch from right next to the dugout. It was the best seat in the house. After that when I went to the games I bought a bleacher seat instead of sneaking in. I felt I sorta owed it to him. I'd go looking for him to say hello, and then one day he told me about the garden and asked if I wanted to help. It wasn't far away so I said sure. I had already found this place by then." He looked up at her. "And that's it. I liked him. He was a funny old man but not many woulda done what he did. Really a shame. I don't understand it."

Margaret finished her tea and was silent for a moment. She was reluctant to reveal too much.

"I don't know, Jerry. I thought you might help. Did you notice anything, anything at all? Maybe something with the garden?"

"Suppose it had nothing to do with that. Maybe he bet the games and hit it big—maybe the numbers."

"Maybe. But you see, we all knew him from the garden so that's where I'm starting."

"We?" Jerry looked sharply at her. "You mean Peter and Cecile and the rest. Why us?"

"It's a start." Margaret breathed heavily. "My only one. Listen, Jerry. Do you want to help or not? All I'm asking is whether you noticed anything strange going on in the garden."

"No, nothing . . . ever." He looked at her boldly. "Everyone got along very well together. You knew that. There was always some friendly jiving, but that's all. We all liked the man."

"No arguments?"

"None." He hesitated. "Well, except for the time Luiz got angry at John for leaving the gate unlocked one night."

Margaret frowned. "When was that?"

"Right after the planting, I think. John apologized and that was the end of it. I think you came late that day."

"After the planting, you're sure?"

He nodded. "Yeah. That's right. I remember Luiz saying that we still had some seed left that coulda been stolen. I mean, the door was wide open."

"I see. Anything else?"

"Nope." He finished his candy bar in silence and glanced at the open door. "Will this take much longer, Margaret? I just saw ten dollars go walking by."

"Did the others know Luiz from before like you, or did

any of them just come by the garden and start working?''

"I think Luiz knew Peter. I'm not sure about the others. No one ever mentioned it.''

Margaret smiled and got up. "Thank you, Jerry. You've been very helpful. Remember it's four o'clock this afternoon, not two.''

"Say, what's that got to do with Luiz? Funny how the cops are acting. They usually don't mess with community stuff. You suppose it's connected?''

Margaret tried to look convincing. "I'm sure it isn't,'' she said.

He was halfway through the door when Margaret asked him the last question.

"By the way, Jerry, the brother you live with, what does he do?''

The boy turned halfway toward her.

"Philip? He works down on Forty-seventh Street. He's a diamond setter.''

17

"HORGAN gave us another night," Morley said. "I told him I thought there was stolen merchandise buried somewhere in the garden and that it tied in with the Valdez murder. I was using it as bait."

"You didn't tell him you found the Rosenblatt ice?" Schaeffer asked.

"And get the whole fucking department down here messing around? Hell no. I can always do that after Friday. He finally calmed down. Son-of-a-bitch was hotter than a twenty-dollar gold watch when I walked in."

"Can't blame him, Sam." Schaeffer poured himself a cup of coffee. "Guy's got a political future to think about. This bad press isn't good for him."

"Politics!" Morley looked disgusted. "Sometimes I think that's all they understand up there. They outside?" The sergeant nodded. "Okay, show them in. And keep Dillon out. I got enough problems without him on my case. Ask

Margaret to come back afterwards. I want to have a little chat with her!''

Schaeffer left and in two minutes the ad hoc garden committee came in and sat down. Before anything happened, Mrs. Schwartz took out a small tape recorder and placed it on her lap. She fussed with it for a minute, then looked up.

"What's that for?" Morley asked angrily.

"For my next article. I want to quote you verbatim."

He pointed at it. "You want a meeting, you turn it off."

"Lieutenant Morley, I'm a member of the press and I have my rights. . . ."

"And I have my rights to kick you out of here. Now, what'll it be?" The two glowered at each other for a moment before she reached out a hand and shut it off.

"I thought we were going to get something accomplished here, Lieutenant. You're starting out on the wrong foot."

Margaret interrupted quickly. "Please calm yourselves. It doesn't do anyone any good to get upset. Mrs. Schwartz was only trying to do her job, Lieutenant Morley. Now, I believe you were going to give us some information."

"I thought I could, but the owner has requested to remain anonymous. I'm sorry."

"I'm sorry too!" Mrs. Schwartz said immediately. "Because I happen to know who the owner is. I've done some checking at One Centre Street." All eyes turned toward her. "At the City Real Property Assessment Department. It's public information. I think you'll all be interested to hear."

Morley felt a sinking feeling in his stomach.

"The city," Mrs. Schwartz continued.

"What? . . ."

"That's right. That property was claimed by the city in lieu of back taxes in 1973." She looked around her with the supercilious grin of victory. "Now, perhaps Lieutenant Morley here will be good enough to tell us why the city has locked us out of its own empty lot."

Morley lit a cigarette and tried to remain calm. Goddamn Margaret! The news would hit the papers, but not until the morning. He still had the night. If he caved in now, there was no chance. If he could buy another day . . . Perhaps. It meant toughing it out.

"You better go check again," he said roughly. "You've got the wrong property, lady. Whoever told you that was confused."

"Confused! You deny it then?" She sounded aghast.

"I do. Until you show me proof. Now, as far as I'm concerned, nothing's changed. We close it up tomorrow. You better make sure you're all cleaned out. That's all. Good day." He stood up abruptly.

"Hey, wait a minute," Jerry said. "You're just going to kick us out. That's it?"

"That's right, unless I see some proof."

"The *Times* will hear about this," Mrs. Schwartz said in a high, reedy voice. "I never make mistakes. I double-checked the records."

"I'm sure you did. It's just that I have different information. I'm sorry, folks, I'm a busy man." Without saying another word, he walked out of the room, leaving the little committee silently staring at each other.

"Don't worry, he'll have his proof all right." Mrs. Schwartz's face had lost some of its color. "If that's what the monster wants . . . and a lot more. Maybe it's not too late today." She got up and rushed out of the room.

"Come on, let's go. No use staying here," Jerry said. They filed out of the precinct but a block away Margaret stopped.

"You go ahead. I forgot I have to do an errand. I'll see you in the garden later." She watched them walk away, and when they rounded the corner, she turned and headed back to the precinct.

*   *   *

Morley was waiting for her. His face had assumed a mask-like calm, which he was doing his best to keep intact. Schaeffer was in the chair Mrs. Schwartz had just vacated, head thrown back, eyes closed.

"Come in," Morley offered. "Now that you're unarmed."

"Now, Lieutenant. I can't help it if they asked me to join their group." She walked in and sat down. Fortunately Morley's cigarettes were nearby and she quickly grabbed one. "After all, it would seem strange if I didn't. Everyone knows how much I'm involved."

"You could have gone a little easier on us. Jesus, Margaret, that little busybody Schwartz is wrecking your own operation. The crook hasn't moved because he doesn't think he has to. And you know something"—he pointed a finger at her—"after tomorrow, he may be right."

"Can't you hold out? Close the garden down anyway. Maybe it's just the pressure we need."

Morley frowned. "Are you kidding? Tomorrow morning The *Times* will have it on page one. They'll string us up by our thumbs. And they'll be right. What we've done is lousy, and one very embarrassed Lieutenant Morley is going to have to explain it." He leaned back. "Now you tell me how I can force my way through that and still be able to walk down the street here. And"—he leaned forward again—"that's not taking into consideration the chief of police who will be on the phone tomorrow morning by nine fifteen yelling at me to stop playing cutesy with the community and give them back their garden. All of which will happen if the diamonds aren't lifted tonight." He took a deep breath. "And if you want my opinion, I don't think they will be. Not with all the commotion you've raised. The answer is no, I can't hold out. Not against that. After tomorrow I give you back your garden and resurrect the stones. I'll just have to say it was all a mistake."

Margaret was silent for a minute, studying the glowing end of her cigarette. When she spoke again, it was in a soft voice, low enough to cause Schaeffer to open his eyes and lean forward.

"One needn't follow the other."

"What?"

"Give them back the garden, but leave the stones buried."

The two policemen looked at each other in disbelief.

"Margaret, that's a quarter of a million dollars in stolen merchandise. You want us to walk away from it. In a virtually open garden?" Schaeffer sounded surprised.

"Maybe Margaret thinks I can keep a round-the-clock stake on it for the next month. Like we have nothing else to do around here."

"You don't have to keep a lookout. . . . No reason to." Margaret frowned. "After all this, the crook will feel perfectly safe leaving them where they are. Going after them now after all that commotion would be too risky. If anything, he'll dig them up at the very end of the harvest season. As long as the plants are growing it's a perfect cover for him. Besides, in another few weeks that open area will be filled in with new vines from the nearby cucumbers. He'll wait. It's only logical."

"It's also logical to give them back to their owners," Morley said.

"Lieutenant Morley. Can't you be serious for a moment?"

"Be serious!"

"Just listen. How many people know about the diamonds. I mean, besides Bertie and me?"

Morley hesitated, as though answering her question would undermine his decision. "Why?"

"How many?" she pressed. "Stop being so cautious."

He shrugged. "Just Schaeffer and me. Jacobson and Staunton were told it was something valuable . . . that's all. But I don't see—"

"So if we leave the stones there for a while no one's going to give you any trouble. I mean the insurance company or the people investigating the robbery?"

"No," Morley said, "but we're not going to leave the stones there for a while. Either the crook gets them tonight, or Schaeffer gets them in the morning. You should only know the problems they're having over Rosenblatt down in Midtown North. No clues, nothing. They got maybe four men on it full time and here I'm sitting on the stuff."

"I know, Lieutenant, the taxpayer always comes first." She looked at him and shook her head sadly. "I'm surprised at you. Really I am. If you give them back the stones, what will that do? It won't catch the thief, you know there are no prints on the box, and it certainly won't solve Luiz's murder. All it will do is save the insurance company some money. They're all a bunch of tightwads anyway. What I had to go through with Oscar's little policy . . ." She sat back. "No, Lieutenant, you're giving up too easily. Especially if no one's forcing you. Now, here's how I figure it. It's gotta be one of the five kids. Chances are I can scare whoever it is into moving, but I need time, and I need the stones left where they are. If the police can't do it with a general closing, I can do it with an on-the-spot threat."

"How do you know it's one of the kids?" Schaeffer asked. "That lock's a cinch to pick. Anyone could have gotten in."

Margaret turned toward him. "Because of the timing. Luiz was murdered the night he was going to check out the garden. Why just then? Because the crook found out about Luiz's suspicions only that afternoon, and he found out because Luiz was acting so strange in the garden. I remember he even dragged me over and pointed excitedly to the cucumbers. The murderer must have seen him and become frightened. All five of them were working at that moment in the garden. So it had to be one of them; no one else would have

become alarmed." She leaned forward and pulled out a cigarette. "Do you mind?"

Morley waved her ahead. He had his hand over his mouth
and was studying her.

"I think that whoever it was had to make sure and followed Luiz home. Luiz let him in innocently—I remember
the door was open—and mentioned his suspicions. It must
have been someone he believed he could trust. The thief then
felt he had no alternative. So he simply killed Luiz. An old
man, expendable, who would care? The only person to worry
about then would be me, and as you know, I look as
harmless as a butterfly." She took a puff of the cigarette and
smiled at Morley. "What do you think so far?"

He just shook his head slowly. "Go ahead."

"I started doing some investigating. Remember there are
only five people involved. That narrowed the field down and
makes it all so much easier. Two things: Luiz had a bit of an
argument with one of the kids about leaving the gate unlocked one night . . . John Kee. He could have been setting
it up to do the burial later that night. Also, Jerry's brother
works in the diamond business. You see what I'm driving at.
I could be very discreet in my inquiries. It's one of them and
it shouldn't be too difficult to find out which one. But that's
not enough. We've got to catch him with the stones."

Morley got up and walked to the window.

"Margaret, you're asking me to stick my neck out a yard.
For what?"

"For the memory of a decent old man who only had good
in his heart, who loved the underprivileged kids in this city
and was killed because of it. Maybe you can turn your back
on that, but I can't. He was my friend."

"Besides," Schaeffer added, "your neck's already
stretched out."

Morley glared at him. "Who asked you?"

"Come on, Sam, give her another chance. It's not like

anyone else knows about those rocks. If it weren't for Margaret you never would have seen them in the first place."

"And, if you're worried about me," Margaret added, "I can take care of myself."

"Yeah, I'll bet," Morley said. He came back to the desk and sat down. He made a big commotion of shuffling papers around. Schaeffer realized it was all a stall.

"Well?" Margaret asked.

"Okay, okay. You can have two weeks. Not a day more. And if you're so hot for this plan, Schaeffer, you can keep an eye on her."

"Thank you." Margaret stood up. "I'd also like to talk to the dealer who was robbed—Rosenblatt. I mean not officially. Could you get me an address?"

"I guess so," Morley growled. "Why do you want to see him?"

"Merely background."

He shook his head. "I don't know how you do it, Margaret, but you always seem to get around me. I coulda said no. What would you have done?"

She smiled. "You mean after you realized I was prepared to go to Mrs. Schwartz with the full story."

Morley frowned. "You wouldn't have!"

"Good-bye, Lieutenant. Let's still hope for the best tonight. I'll call." Very quickly Margaret opened the door and walked out. She heard Sergeant Schaeffer's low-pitched laugh all the way out to the front hall.

The *Times* did have it, and on page one. But Morley was wrong about the time. Horgan called at 8:30 the next morning, not 9:15. If the lieutenant wasn't quite awake when he picked up the phone, he was a minute later. He just listened, said a few Yes, sirs, and waited. Finally Horgan took a breath.

"All right, I'll notify the press," Morley ventured.

"They'll be glad to hear we're not closing it. I had hoped—"
But his explanation was cut short by a string of Horgan's
choicest phrases. It was all he could do to get off the phone
in one piece. He waited until 9:00, then called the three daily
papers and made the briefest of explanations. By 9:30 it was
all over. He sent one of the patrol cars over to notify anyone
at the garden site about the change in plans and pin up a new
notice. At 9:45 Margaret called to get the news and also
Rosenblatt's address. Morley hung the phone up with a soft
curse and treated himself to a cup of coffee. Then he tried to
forget the whole thing.

18

MARGARET waited until after working hours to make the trip. Brooklyn had always been a mystery to her and it was worse at dark. There were a hundred different neighborhoods, a hundred different main streets, and a hundred ways of getting lost. Margaret found one of them. The street Rosenblatt was supposed to live on came to an abrupt end two hundred numbers before his address. She couldn't find a trace of it resuming anywhere nearby and tried a bus. Nothing. Finally she was about to give up when she spotted another version of the street she was looking for. She hopped out of the bus and found herself just a few doors away from the address. That had happened to her before in Brooklyn. Streets mysteriously sprang into and out of existence and finding one's way around was always something of a personal victory. Margaret walked the few yards and entered the lobby of the gem dealer's building.

Immediately she was set back forty years. It was the kind of building that was its own neighborhood. Large, formerly on the luxurious side, it now housed the equivalent of a small town in Eastern Europe, including its heavy smells of cabbage, potatoes, and old furs. This was real Social Security Brooklyn. Margaret figured the median age would be around seventy-two. Good, she'd fit right in. She stood by the interior door fumbling conspicuously in her big handbag until some resident who was on his way out graciously let her in. She thanked him politely, snapped her bag shut, and took the elevator upstairs to the Rosenblatt apartment. She rang the bell and waited.

Fortunately for her, Mrs. Rosenblatt opened the door and smiled pleasantly. She was not a thin woman, but whatever bulk she had seemed to be lost in the large dress she was wearing. Her hair was covered by a fine net that stopped just above her ears. In one hand she held a dish towel. Margaret held a can timidly in front of her in a way she thought would be most unthreatening. She was wearing her most conservative suit, a dark blue cotton she had just purchased at Loehmann's. She returned the smile and introduced herself.

"Hello, I'm Sadie Lowe from the building . . . collecting for the Hadassah fair."

It took only a second. "A Hadassah fair? But I hadn't heard. Come in, come in. From walking these halls you must be tired. I'm Hazel Rosenblatt."

Margaret thanked her and in another minute was sitting in her living room describing the wonderful things they were going to do with the proceeds from the fair.

"So how come is it I haven't heard? The east side of this building is like Siberia. The news we get is already like last week's knishes." Mrs. Rosenblatt shook her head. "You live maybe near Mrs. Finkel . . . twelve-C?"

Margaret shook her head. "I just moved in last month so I don't know too many people yet. Is that the woman with the walker?"

"No, no, that's Mrs. Horshstein." Mrs. Rosenblatt looked

at Margaret more closely. "I was wondering how is it I hadn't seen you before in the lobby."

"Who's that?" a loud voice asked from the other room.

"Mrs. Lowe from the building, Abie. Come in."

An older man wearing bedroom slippers and a gray cardigan shuffled in. "From the building?" He held out his hand slowly.

"My husband," Hazel Rosenblatt introduced. "Just finishing a little nap. Sit, Abie, Mrs. Lowe is collecting for Hadassah."

"Always a pleasure to meet neighbors," the gem dealer said, and sat on the couch next to her. In a minute they were chatting about the building.

"Have you lived here a long time?" Margaret asked.

"Fifteen years. Moved over from the Concourse," Hazel said.

"Such a nice building," Margaret continued, unobtrusively placing the can with the Hadassah emblem by her side. "So safe. Not like Manhattan."

"Manhattan. Don't get me started," Mr. Rosenblatt said. "See this scar . . ." And he leaned forward to show her the top of his head. Margaret frowned sympathetically and settled herself back into her seat.

"How did you ever get that?"

"You wouldn't believe me if I told you," he said. Margaret's eyes opened wide. It was the only invitation he needed to spend the next ten minutes describing the robbery in detail.

"Abie, you're boring Mrs. Lowe," his wife broke in. "She came to collect for Hadassah, not to hear about our problems."

"No, Mrs. Rosenblatt, I had no idea. I think I read something in the paper about it. But didn't the police ever find him? I thought he left some clues."

"Clues, shmoos. Nothing. I don't even know if it was a

man or woman. The voice was deliberately muffled. Then I got hit so fast I didn't see a thing. I started to turn around, next thing I know I was on the floor.''

"Abie," Hazel interrupted, "didn't you say whoever it was had on sneakers?''

"Yes. I told the police that. 'So, big deal,' they said. 'Only two million people in New York got on sneakers.' ''

Margaret cleared her throat. "How did you know he wore sneakers?''

"I guess just a split second before I blacked out, while I was on the floor I musta seen the feet. I couldn't see any more because I couldn't lift my head.''

"And you're sure there was only one of them?''

Abe Rosenblatt looked at his wife. It was a moment before he answered. "Well, I was positive until I was hit. Walking down the corridor I felt there was only one. It's what I told the police. But then, when I woke up in the hospital room, I had this funny feeling . . .''

"Yes?''

"Well, just that there were two of them. I don't understand it. I even remember only one pair of sneakers.'' He shrugged. "I think I must've been dreaming then.''

"All you saw was feet?'' Margaret looked puzzled.

"That's right.''

"Can I get you some coffee, Mrs. Lowe?'' the other woman interrupted. "I'm afraid I'm not being a very good hostess.''

"Yes, thank you.'' Mrs. Rosenblatt left the room and Margaret straightened out her skirt.

"You have no idea then who it might have been?'' She looked back at the man. "I mean one would think that it must have been someone in the industry, someone who knew you would be carrying so many valuable stones.''

"That's not hard to figure out. Every day for me it's the same routine. In the morning I pick up from the Diamond

Dealers Club on Forty-seventh Street and in the evening I put back. You understand they're not my stones, I just act as a broker on commission. So I go to maybe ten firms a day, mostly in the district, and by now even the policeman's horse on the block knows my face. Forty-two years is a long time. Besides," he added, "you carry a black bag with a chain to your wrist and people aren't going to think you're peddling ball-point pens. You know what I mean."

Margaret nodded. "So then it didn't have to be necessarily someone in the diamond business?"

"That's right. Coulda been a janitor in one of the buildings. Sometimes I go to the same one twice a day." He threw up his hand. "Coulda been anybody."

Mrs. Rosenblatt came back with the cups.

"Such a *meshuggeneh* business," she said. "The diamonds shouldn't travel, the buyers should."

"Then I'd be out of a job."

"But not hit over the head and almost killed."

"Ach," he said. "You can't figure it. My brother's a cabdriver and he's been robbed four times. So"—he looked at Margaret—"what's the answer?"

"Florida," Hazel Rosenblatt said and poured the coffee. "If you weren't so stubborn. I hear you can even get a good challa down there." Margaret didn't say anything and let the conversation drift for a few minutes.

"You know," she finally said. "I bet it was some kid." She turned to Mrs. Rosenblatt. "They're always doing such terrible things. Awful the way youth has become. And the sneakers sound right."

"Maybe," Mr. Rosenblatt said, jumping over the last few minutes of chitchat without hesitation.

"So stop it already." Hazel looked at her husband scornfully. "As it is you don't get any sleep at night thinking about it."

"I'm sorry," Margaret said. "I'm afraid I'm too

curious.'' She finished her coffee. ''You will come to the fair?''

''But of course. You'll drop off a notice?''

Margaret nodded, and as she did, she felt Hazel Rosenblatt lean over and drop some change in the can. ''Something extra.'' The woman smiled.

Margaret got up and made her way to the door.

''Thank you. You've been very kind.''

''Do come again, and if you see Mrs. Horshstein in the lobby tell her the Mah-Jongg is this Thursday.''

Margaret closed the door behind her and walked slowly to the elevator.

19

"HAVE you ever had Thunderbird wine?" Margaret asked. They were sitting on a bench on one of the islands in the middle of Broadway—the one on Eighty-second to be exact, Bertie's favorite.

Bertie shook her head. "You mean that stuff Roosa drinks?" She chuckled. "Red lightning, he calls it. No, never had the nerve. Of course I'll have a glass of sherry now and then—mind you only for digestion."

"And Manhattans." Margaret smiled.

"Oh, well, just to be sociable." Bertie straightened out her sweater. "Why?"

"Nothing," Margaret said casually. "Just curious."

Bertie reached into the paper bag on her lap and took out a handful of crumbs. Immediately the ten pigeons that were coyly waiting on the fringes of the island came hobbling over. The routine was always the same; she threw a straight line of crumbs in front of her and then a few handfuls to each side. After a minute she pointed to one of the birds.

"Samson's looking better this week. Must be the weather." Bertie shifted on the bench and leaned closer. She lowered her voice. "I'm dying to know what it's all about. It's difficult for me, Margaret, not being able to mention it to a soul. And so exciting too."

"I told you." Margaret frowned. "You'll just get me in trouble. Soon as I find out anything I'll let you know."

"Promise?"

"I promise."

Bertie threw out another handful of crumbs and watched as the birds squabbled over them.

"How you gonna find out?"

"I don't have the faintest idea." She looked at her watch. "Anyway, Bertie, I'll see you later." She got up. "Right now I've got to go to the garment center."

"Buying something?" Bertie asked.

"No." Margaret smiled. "Just trying on."

C and J Casuals had the smallest waiting room she had ever seen, and half of it was taken up with a dusty plastic philodendron. She approached the receptionist and tapped softly on the glass. It took a few seconds for the woman to realize that the tapping was not coming from the offices or cutting room behind her. She looked up from the paperback book she was reading and fixed Margaret with a lazy stare.

"Yes?"

"I'd like to speak to Peter Muñoz please."

"Who?"

Margaret repeated the name, raising her voice to overcome the noises from the factory.

"Sorry, no one here like that."

"But he just told me the other day. He's a young boy, about seventeen, curly hair, fancy dresser."

"Oh, Pedro!" The receptionist smiled. "Whyn'tcha say so. Yeah, he works the racks. Hold on." She got up and walked to the rear. A minute later Peter poked his head out through the doorway.

"Margaret!"

"I missed you yesterday at the garden."

He shifted from one foot to the other. "Yeah, I came late. That's something about the reopening."

"I wanted to ask you some questions, Peter. Luiz is dead." She watched his reaction.

"I heard. Jerry told me." He looked over his shoulder. "Listen, Margaret, I gotta run. I got this rush delivery to make. Talk to you tonight?"

"I'll come along," she said. "If you don't mind, that is. You're walking?"

He nodded and after a moment's hesitation opened the door wider. "Okay, come on." She followed him into the factory and over to the shipping department. There were racks and racks of dresses of all colors and styles. Peter wheeled an empty rack over and began transferring some of the dresses. He held the shipping invoice in his hand and checked off the items he had moved.

"The cruise line," he said. "Don't know why they're in such a rush for it. It's still the summer." When he finished, he wheeled the loaded cart over to the elevator and pushed the button. In a few seconds the door opened and Peter and Margaret entered.

"What'd you want to know?"

"What happened."

"And you think I can help?"

"Maybe. Maybe you saw something. Maybe he told you something."

Peter shook his head. "If he had, I woulda remembered." The doors opened and he moved the cart forward onto the street. "Come on, we gotta hustle. Traffic out here is murder. Stay in one place too long and they just shove you out of the way. They overturned a whole cart on me one day." He

started off down the block at a pace that had Margaret nearly
trotting. When they came to Sixth Avenue, they had to wait
for the light.

"Whew." She breathed hard. "You do this every day?"

"Yeah. It's a pain, ain't it? Job's for the birds. I can't wait
until I get me some real bread and won't have to hustle so
much." He smiled. "What I get from them just about pays
for the shoe shines."

"You got another job?" Margaret looked puzzled.

"I'm working on it."

Margaret paused for a deep breath, then looked up at him
again. "Peter, how did you meet Luiz?"

He tugged at one of the plastic bags keeping the dresses in
place. "Does it matter?"

"It might. Did you know him before the garden?"

He looked at her with surprise. "Where you think I'd meet
a nice old dude like that, at some disco shakin' his thing?"
He smirked. "Unh-unh. We didn't exactly work the same
ends of the street."

"Then you never saw him before?"

Peter looked at the light anxiously.

"Yeah, I'd seen him once or twice. I gotta be straight with
you. The man's dead, right. Don't want to tell no lies gonna
get me in trouble."

"Where?"

He hesitated. "At church. Usta go to the same place up on
129th Street. All Saints—when my mother was still alive. I
never talked to him. Sometimes she would, but I remembered
the face. Then one day, I'm walking and I see this old guy
clearing a lot. He stands up and it's him." He shrugged.
"That's how it started."

"I see. But it doesn't explain why you decided to work
there."

"Simple. My old lady died. They were friends. I figured
I'd help him . . . for her." The light changed and Peter

pushed ahead. All sorts of horns were honking on either side of them, but they made it through the intersection without incident. Margaret followed as he maneuvered the cart skillfully between two double-parked cars and then brought it up onto the sidewalk.

"That is quite simple," she said. "Almost too much so. Just because they were friends?"

"Yeah, why not? Only mother I had."

Margaret changed the subject. "How about the other kids? Did any know him from before like you?"

"Jerry did. Luiz used to tell me about Jerry and the ball games. Don't know about Vinnie or John. Cecile, well that's another story."

"What do you mean?"

Peter pulled back on the cart just in time to avoid a sidewalk trapdoor gate that was beginning to open. He forced his rack around it and kept going.

"One day she just appeared. Never said nothing to no one. Kind of like a ghost. Unfriendly too. I put a few moves on her . . ." He stopped and looked at Margaret appraisingly.

She nodded. "I understand. You wanted to keep company. Go ahead."

"Anyway I coulda been a light switch during the blackout: no response. Like that with all the others. Even with Luiz and he was always trying to be nice. We all figured the chick had some heavy scene at home so we stayed outta her way."

Margaret blinked. "Then you don't think she knew Luiz from before."

"No," he said. "No way. I'd bet on it." Just then an attractive young woman walked past them and Peter interrupted himself to look. He said something in Spanish and the girl turned and smiled.

"Wait here," Peter ordered Margaret. "Do me a favor and hold the cart."

He leapt away and spun through the other pedestrians until

he caught up with the girl as she turned the corner. Reluctantly, Margaret pushed the cart over to the side and waited. Five minutes later Peter was back with a broad grin on his face.

"Can't keep them away. Hey, you coming?" He guided the rack into one of the buildings as Margaret hurried in behind him.

"*Muchas gracias,*" he said. "Now I got a question for you." His eyes narrowed. "How come you're so interested?"

Margaret was silent for a minute.

"He was my friend. Like he was your mother's." She leaned a hand against the cart and looked closely into his eyes. There was a moment of uneasy silence.

"Supposed to have been a robbery," Peter said and Margaret detected the slightest nervousness in his voice.

"That's what I've been trying to find out." She smiled and it broke the tension. "And you've been very helpful, Peter. Thank you."

"It's a shame. Luiz was okay, man, a real *compadre.*" He gave the rack a shove and followed it into the open elevator. Then he turned. Margaret had a last glimpse of his handsome face with its jet black hair as the doors closed.

20

Soon after Margaret arrived at the garden that afternoon, the sky turned an iron gray and in no time sheets of rain swept the plot, creating large puddles. Well and good for the vegetables, Margaret thought, but not for my shoes. The garden was empty and the door locked. She hurried to a nearby coffee shop to wait out the downpour.

She was more than surprised to see Sergeant Schaeffer there, looking for all the world like he was expecting her. He waved and motioned her over. He was dressed in his usual blue jeans and open shirt, and his beard looked a little more unkempt than the last time she'd seen him. In fact she thought he looked downright exhausted, and wasted no time in telling him so.

"It's all these late nights," he said, "and early mornings."

"You ought to complain, David. You need your sleep. You look like Jimmy Stewart in the last reel of *Mr. Smith Goes to Washington.*"

"That bad, huh?" He grinned and took a mouthful of coffee. "The taxpayers want their money's worth. So . . . ." He looked up. "Did he tell you anything?"

"Who?"

"Muñoz."

"How did you know?" All of a sudden it registered. His presence at the sandwich shop, the fresh cup of coffee in front of him. "David, you've been following me!"

"Here and there. Only I wish you wouldn't leave your apartment so early."

"Why?" She sounded hurt. "Nothing's going to happen to me."

"It's just that when you're into one of your little detective numbers I like to keep an eye on you."

"Little detective numbers. Humph!" She snorted. "I'm surprised at you. You could at least have let me know."

"I am."

"Well, I don't like it. Not at all." She frowned. "I want you to stop." She called a waitress over and ordered a tea. "Just because I'm old enough to be your mother, David, you mustn't think I'm some helpless old biddy."

"No." He smiled. "I don't. But I do worry."

"Well, I don't like having a shadow." She sat back in her seat. "It makes it difficult for me to do my job."

He took a big sip of coffee to hide the grin.

"Well?" she demanded.

"Okay," he said. "I'll stop. Only, call me every day, or else I'll really worry. Now," he asked, "what did Muñoz tell you?"

"Muñoz?" She smiled innocently. "Nothing really. But then I didn't expect him to. Or any of them for that matter. I'm just after impressions."

Schaeffer shook his head. "You going to catch a murderer on impressions?"

"Of course not." Her eyes sparkled. "I told you, the murderer is going to catch himself. You'll see."

Schaeffer sipped his coffee slowly. "Who's next on your list?"

"I was hoping to see Vincent Tortelli."

"The kid with the record?"

"What record?"

"What record!" Schaeffer shook his head. "Margaret, if you're going to do detective work don't forget the basics. Tortelli's got the only sheet in the lot. Coupla petty larcenies, one liquor store, one mugging."

"Vinnie?"

"Yeah, sweet Vinnie. Thought you should know. He hangs out in a bad crowd, up on West 111th. It's hard to know how he got sucked in, but he's there."

"A big gang?"

"No, pretty small as I understand it. Loose, stays on the fringes. Now and then they try something stupid. Tortelli's kind of their mascot . . . everyone's little brother. Consequently, he got tabbed as the lookout, and that's how he got collared every time. You'd think he would have learned."

"You would, yes." Margaret frowned. "Well, I'll have to talk to him. Maybe I can help." She looked out the window at the rain. "But not in this. He won't be out."

"No. Who else is there?"

"Maybe John Kee." She searched in her big handbag until she pulled out a card, "Yes, here it is. 'Ace Refrigeration and Heating School . . . No High School Diploma Necessary.' "

"He a student there?"

"Studying air conditioning I think. He gave me this last week. It's not far." She looked up. "Mind you, I don't want company. If you want to make yourself really useful you can check out Philip Stein, Jerry's brother."

"His brother?"

"The one in the diamond business." She gave Schaeffer a pleasant little smile and got up from the table.

"Thanks for the coffee, and David"—she waved her finger—"get some sleep."

21

THE Ace Refrigeration and Heating School was located upstairs in one of the older office buildings on Broadway in the
seventies. Their hand-lettered sign looked very impressive on
the plate glass doorway and obscured the imprint of a former
tenant, the Ace Typing and Steno School. Margaret pushed
her way in, shook the rain off her hat, and looked
around. She was greeted by a tiny space with white walls, an
immaculate floor, and a table full of registration forms. A
bell must have announced her presence, for within a minute
another door opened and a short man walked in. Margaret
couldn't help thinking how much he looked like Dominic, the
superintendent in her building.

"Can I help you?" he asked.

"I'm looking for John Kee. I believe he is one of your
students." The man gave Margaret a quick once-over and
told her curtly to step inside.

"He's very busy now. He's in a freon lecture."

"This won't take a minute."

He led her through the large main workroom, past tables

piled high with copper tubing, aluminum fins, strips of fiber glass, and multicolored electric wires. There were only a few people working, usually in groups of two or three. Most of them were in their teens or early twenties. The two instructors Margaret noticed were both in white laboratory coats and she thought looked suspiciously like the actor George Sanders, very professional but strangely imposterish. Overall there was the hum of motors and the smell of oil. She followed the short man into a corner of the loft where a section had been walled off. Behind it was a blackboard, half a dozen chairs, and one large table. Posed in front of the blackboard was another white-coated instructor glancing through a book. John Kee was in the nearest chair.

"Hello, Margaret." He looked surprised.

"Hello, John. Can you spare a few minutes?"

The boy looked quickly at the instructor, who was still searching for something in the book.

"Sure, what's up?"

Margaret motioned and walked a few steps into the other room. She cleared a small space on one of the cluttered tables and set her handbag down. It took her only a few seconds to find her cigarettes.

"Don't think that's such a good idea," John said quickly. "There's a lot of gases around."

"Oh, sorry," Margaret said and put the matches back. She closed her handbag slowly and turned back to him.

"John, I want to know what you and Luiz quarreled about."

"Quarreled?" The boy looked confused. "We didn't quarrel." He thought for a moment. "Oh, you mean about locking the door." His round eyes narrowed. "That was nothing. A misunderstanding. I was the last person to leave that night, but I remembered distinctly locking the gate, just like I always do. Luiz was upset because the next morning he found it open."

"You're sure you locked it?"

"Yes. Someone else must have come in after I left and forgot to close it."

Margaret thought for a minute. "You've never given your key to anyone, have you? I mean even for a couple of hours."

"Never. It's right on my key ring." He pulled it out to show her. "It's always with me." He closed a fist around the keys. "What's this all about, Margaret? And where's Luiz? With what's been happening at the garden . . ."

She told him as briefly as she could. "It was in the paper three days ago. I guess you didn't see it." She noticed his eyes glisten over. "I'm sorry, John. I'm trying to find out why it happened."

"And you thought I . . ."

"I thought you might have had bad feelings. That's all. I can see I was wrong."

John looked down at the floor for a full minute. Margaret could tell he was trying to control his emotions.

"He was a very special person." He looked up and Margaret could see redness in his eyes.

"Yes, he was." Margaret reached into her handbag again and brought out a Kleenex. She handed it to him and watched as he blew his nose. "It sounds like you knew him from before the garden."

"Yes, for over two years. I used to work with my parents in their vegetable store up in Harlem. Luiz came by once a week to buy his vegetables. He would stop and talk to me all the time, tell me how he used to have his own farm in Puerto Rico, show me what to look for between a good vegetable and a bad one. Things weren't going so well for Mom and Pop in the store so they didn't have much time for me. I'd always look forward to his visit."

"And then he asked you to join him in his own garden?"

John nodded. "Just about the time I decided to come here

to the school. There was no real future in the vegetable stand but Luiz made his garden sound so . . . special. I mean, seeing things grow. I couldn't resist. It was sort of a hobby to me."

She looked around at the school. "And do you like this place?"

John shifted on his feet. "It's a way to make money. Good money." He looked up and a kind of resolve crossed his face. "I don't mind telling you, Margaret, things are bad at home. They lost the vegetable stand and now there's little money coming in. Just some odd jobs my dad gets unloading up at the Hunts Point market. But the real trouble is—" he hesitated, "—my dad promised to bring his brother and his family over from Korea. He gave his word, and now there's no way." He looked at her closely. "Imagine how he feels now, Margaret. The family pooled all their savings in Korea so that we could come over. We were to lead the way." He laughed bitterly to himself. Slowly the laughter gave way to a look of determination. "So I've got to do something— anything—to get my uncle over here. It's up to me. My father's too humiliated at the loss of their savings. Do you understand? It's a matter of honor, not of whether I like this place or not."

"I understand." She nodded. "I hope you're good at it at least?" Margaret held up an electronic component from the cluttered table, one with three or four switches and a dozen colored wires coming out of it. "It all looks so complicated."

He smiled thinly. "That's just a sophisticated thermostat. It's not hard if you know how to connect it. It's as easy as replacing a light bulb."

"I see." Margaret lowered the part. "And this?" She pointed to a little clearing on the bench where a single tool lay.

"Just a screwdriver." He shrugged.

"With that funny end?"

"It's a Phillips screwdriver. Mostly for sheet-metal screws. We use it all the time." John turned in the direction of the classroom. Margaret noticed the instructor walking toward them.

"One more question," she said quickly. "Do you know if Cecile or Vinnie knew Luiz before the garden began?"

John shook his head. "I couldn't say. Cecile always seemed to have a chip on her shoulder and didn't talk much. Vinnie, yeah, I think he did mention something. Had to do with baseball." He thought for a minute. "Or stickball. But it's all I can remember. Ask Vinnie."

"I will."

The instructor tapped John on the arm. "We're waiting, Mr. Kee. I don't think you should miss this."

John took a step back. "I've got to go, Margaret. I'm awfully sorry about Luiz."

"I understand," Margaret said. "We all are."

He turned and followed the instructor back into the classroom. She listened to the sound of the rubber soles of his sneakers squeaking on the white linoleum floor behind him. Then she took a last look at the thermostat, and walked out.

22

SHE was surprised to see that it was only 3:30 as she left the building. The rain was still coming down and collecting in the gutters. The wisest thing would have been to go home, but her apartment in the afternoon always seemed so lonely, more so than in the evenings. There was only one place to go. She walked quickly and caught the uptown bus that let her off at her favorite indoor gossip place, the Flora K. Bliss Community Center. She could always count on someone she knew being there, especially when it rained and the benches on Broadway were empty. Today was no different. As she stepped into the vestibule, she saw her friend Rose just entering the little cafeteria. Margaret quickly hung her coat up and walked after her.

The room was not crowded, but at least three people waved at Margaret. She went over to each one to say hello and only then did she get her tea and find Rose in the corner of the room. Rose's shopping bags were spread out around her two deep and a magazine was open on the table next to her. She was studying it closely. Margaret noticed that it was a Bloomingdale's white-sale catalogue from last Columbus Day. She set her cup down noisily and dropped into the next seat.

"Hello, Rose. Nasty day out."

The other woman looked up, a bit startled, but when she saw who it was, her face relaxed.

" 'Lo, Margaret." She slurped some coffee from her cup. "Ain't it. Everything's so wet." She glanced down quickly at her bags. "Figured I'd catch my death of cold out there."

Margaret nodded at the catalogue. "Where'd you find that?"

"This?" Rose closed it and pushed it a few inches farther away. "Had it for a while. Got some nice pictures, but you oughta see those prices. It's enough to make a body think twice about bathing. Ten dollars for a towel." She snorted. "Never heard of such a thing."

Margaret laughed. "Inflation."

Rose dropped the catalogue back into one of the bags and eyed Margaret more closely. "Next thing you know it'll be five dollars for a bar of soap. Then we'll all be in trouble."

"I suppose so," Margaret said and ladled two spoons of sugar into her cup. Rose was silent for a minute; her eyes were on Margaret's hand as it stirred the tea.

"Margaret," she began, and her voice had a different, a hesitant quality to it. "I meant to tell you something. . . . Something I saw. Maybe you should know about it." Rose looked around her carefully as though she expected someone would grab her any minute. "Something about the garden."

Margaret leaned forward. She was always falling for Rose's dramatic flair. Her friend's imagination colored all her stories—like the time she had reported hearing the murder of a child in the basement of an abandoned building, and when the two of them went to check, all they found was a hungry cat.

"What was it?" she said slowly. "Another animal?"

Rose shook her head. "No, this time I seen it plain as day. I mean even though it was pretty dark with it being past midnight."

"What were you doing out past midnight?"

"Ain't unusual for me. Sometimes I can't get to sleep in one spot—too busy maybe—so I move to another. Well, see, that's what happened two, three nights ago. I was walking over to the Ninety-eighth Street twenty-four-hour washateria when I see I'm passing your garden. Don't give it another thought 'cept something catches my eye. Now you know, Margaret, I ain't particularly nosy . . . but it was strange, see, someone digging and such past midnight."

"Digging?" Margaret's eyes opened wider.

"Well, I couldn't be sure. He was bending over and every now and then I caught sight of the streetlight reflecting against something metal. Maybe one of them little hand shovels. I was on the other side of the street but I tell you I could see clear as day. And he was acting mighty suspicious if you ask me. Every minute or two he stops what he's doing and looks over his shoulder. I guess he don't see me for a while 'cause he keeps going. Anyway, I'm trying to make up my mind what to do and I guess on one of his look-sees he spots me. Next thing I know he's disappeared. Hiding I suppose behind some of them tallish plants at the back."

"The corn?"

"Yeah. So I wait another few minutes but he don't come out. I sure ain't goin' in. Nothing to do but keep walking." Rose finished her coffee. "But I had to tell you, Margaret, seeing as how you been so concerned with it and all."

Margaret kept her eyes on her friend for a full half minute before speaking.

"Where was he? I mean in the garden: up front or towards the rear?"

"I guess he was just in front of the corn, or whatever them plants were. Over towards the left a bit. He was on his hands and knees, and as I was watching he was working his way towards the center."

"He didn't stay in one spot?"

Rose shook her head. "Nope. Musta moved ten feet in the time I was watching."

Margaret thought carefully. The corn was at the back of the plot so as not to block the light for the other plants. What was the next row forward? It took her only a few seconds to realize that the intruder had been in the cucumbers. She had a horrible feeling, as though all the air had been sucked from her lungs.

"When was this?"

"Like I said, two, three nights ago. Right after the police reopened the garden. You remember all that fuss. . . ."

Margaret's feeling of confusion deepened. Why, she thought. There was no reason to remove the diamonds. Then she thought of Morley and gave out an involuntary "oh."

"What was that?" Rose squinted.

"Nothing." Maybe by some miracle the stones were still there. Maybe whoever it was only came to check on their safety. She had to look.

"Thank goodness you told me, Rose." She pushed herself back from the table and was about to get up. Her friend frowned.

"Don't you want to know who it was?"

This time Margaret's breath really did catch in her throat.

"You mean you saw?"

"Told you it was clear as day to me, didn't I? 'Course I saw. He looked around enough. It was one of your helpers. Little white boy. Runs around all the time with that dirty sweat shirt, one with that old man's face plastered on it. That's who it was.''

''Jerry?'' Margaret tried to sound casual. ''Same sweat shirt?''

''Yeah.'' Rose frowned. ''I ain't no expert, mind you, but I think it was that fella Beethoven.''

23

THIS time she'd do it alone. No Bertie to hold the flashlight. She knew exactly where the stones were buried and it would take no more than fifteen minutes. The rain had stopped around eight o'clock but by the time she let herself into the garden two hours later, the ground was still wet and the plants dripping. A clean, organic smell rose out of the earth and mingled with the faint ground mist. The sound of a lone cricket came to her from somewhere ahead, a strange noise in the middle of the city. It stopped as she approached and made the turn into the row of cucumbers. Now only the sound of the rustling of the plants as she passed them broke the stillness. That and the occasional car horn from somewhere down the block. Margaret found the spot and very carefully began digging.

Why Jerry? she wondered. She went over their conversation again but it still didn't make any sense. Unless it was the brother, the mysterious diamond setter.

The damp earth gave way easily to Margaret's shovel and

in ten minutes she struck something hard. The dull metallic sound brought her back from her thoughts and she responded by digging faster. In another minute she had it uncovered. Even through the mud-splattered sides she knew she was holding the same box with the diamonds. She gave it a shake and heard the scraping of the stones inside. The wind shifted and new noises came to her, apartment noises—refrigerator doors slamming, TV sets. She started reburying the stones but stopped and listened every few seconds. Her shoes were covered with mud and the hem of her dress felt heavy with wetness, but her sense of relief was numbing. In another five minutes she finished and spread the earth evenly on the top. She didn't wait to catch her breath, but hurried out, locked the door, and walked home. A new question bothered her all the way. What had Jerry been doing in the garden after midnight?

24

At 9:30 the next morning the phone rang as Margaret was filling in the last word of the crossword puzzle. She smiled when she noted the time. Ten minutes ahead of her average. But then today's was easy—all about old movies.

"Did I wake you?" Schaeffer said. "I got the information on Philip Stein."

"Go ahead." She pushed *The New York Times* off her lap and reached over to light a cigarette. "Don't tell me he has a record?"

"Nope. You couldn't find a cleaner nose in town. Good credit. Married." She heard some papers rustling over the phone. "Let's see, worked for F and K Engagement Rings since 1972. They say he's a hard worker, honest, etcetera etcetera. Goes to temple every Friday night. You want more?"

"I think that will do." Margaret was frowning. "He doesn't sound right."

"Plus the fact that he was at work during the robbery. I thought I'd save that for last."

"Thanks." There was a silence on the line for a moment. Margaret wondered whether to tell Schaeffer about Rose's story. Not yet, she decided. Too early. And if Morley found out, it would be trouble.

"So, what's on for today?" Schaeffer asked.

"You're not curious or anything, David?"

"Let's just say concerned. You want to be on your own you got to cooperate just a little, huh?"

"Okay, just a little. I'm weeding."

"Weeding? That's all?"

"Well, one can't weed in silence. I suppose there'll be someone there to talk to."

"Of course."

"David, sometimes I don't think you trust me."

He laughed. "About as far as I can throw a twenty-one-inch color Sony. By the way, did you see the Hitchcock last night?"

"A Hitchcock last night! No."

"*Notorious.* I'm surprised at you, Margaret."

"I know. I was so tired from all that running around I went to bed right after dinner. I couldn't keep my eyes open."

"Too bad," he said. "You missed an exciting evening."

"Didn't I though." She said good-bye and hung the phone up slowly.

Margaret was pleased to see both Cecile and Vincent in the garden when she arrived later that morning. Surprisingly, no new recruits had offered themselves as helpers. Even Mrs. Schwartz had moved on to a new crusade, editorializing against pooper-scooper offenders. There were always kibitzers hanging about, but the actual work still fell to the five teen-agers and Margaret.

It was the first day of really bright sunshine they'd had for the past week, and she was delighted to see how much things had grown. The squash and zucchini were already over six inches long and the tomatoes, although still green, were reaching full size. But what especially pleased her were the flowers. The marigolds were in full bloom around the border of the garden, an orange frame to the green hues of the vegetables. And the row of dahlias she had planted were breathtaking. She had done that surreptitiously, squeezing a thin row in between the beans and cucumbers. They had grown over three inches in the past week, and the large buds had just started bursting open, exploding several shades of color in a straight line from wall to wall. They were purely an extravagance and she had confessed her deed with great relish the week before. Now as the sun lit the flowers, she felt a twinge of sorrow. Luiz should have been there, to see all the beauty he helped create. She silently promised him a bouquet, the first one. Just a few days and they'd be perfect. She raised her eyes from the flowers and walked the few yards to where Cecile was working.

"Mind if I help you?" she asked. "It'll go quicker."

The girl shrugged. "Suit yourself." She turned and continued weeding. Half the row of zucchini was already done. Margaret positioned herself a few steps to the right, bent over, and started pulling at the mangy city growths.

"Weeds are having a field day," Cecile said matter-of-factly. "Bugs too."

"Can't help the weeds. I suppose it's time to use that chemical on the bugs. There's a container in the locker over there."

Margaret walked over, fumbled for a minute, then came back with a pint bottle of dark liquid. Cecile's eyes stayed locked on the older woman as she slowly unscrewed the cap and gingerly held it to her nose. In a second her eyes were tearing from the pungent smell and she quickly replaced the top. "Whew, smells like cleaning fluid."

"That stuff's poison," Cecile said disgustedly. "I thought we weren't going to use it."

Margaret looked puzzled. "We might not have any garden at all if we don't." She picked off a small zucchini leaf with two neat holes drilled through the center and held it up.

"I know," Cecile said. "But it's only a percentage. We use that poison and it'll contaminate everything. Damn. Malathion. That stuff's worse than arsenic. Surprised at the old man for buying it." She looked quickly at Margaret. The mention of Luiz seemed to throw an awkwardness over everything. Cecile leaned back on her haunches.

"You heard then," Margaret asked slowly.

"I heard." She turned her face to the side.

Margaret saw her in profile and again noticed the high cheekbones and the defiant chin, all very unnerving in a seventeen-year-old girl. Cecile didn't say anything. She stared straight ahead.

"Did you know him, Cecile, from before the garden?"

The girl turned slowly. Her face was expressionless.

"No. I met him the first day he started working on it. He was putting up the fence and I gave him a hand, that's all. Never saw him before. But he looked friendly." She turned back to the side and bent over. Her fingers wrapped around one of the thicker weeds and pulled on it slowly. "It's too bad. The old man had something. He cared."

"You get along pretty well?"

"Better than I got along with the rest of them—always hustling and jiving. It's amazing he put up with it."

"But there were arguments."

"Had to be arguments. At first everyone wanted to work their own turf. Bunch of little capitalists. He put a stop to that though. Told them they had to work together, that it was a community effort."

"Did anyone object?"

She nodded. "Vinnie was the loudest, but he fell in line. Had to. Luiz wouldn't let anyone work in the garden otherwise. About time they all got a little education."

"Education?"

"Yeah, politics. None of them gives a damn. None of them trying to understand." Her eyes turned cold.

"What kind of politics?"

"The kind that keeps money in this country moving in one direction—upwards. They didn't care. They're all into their own little blinds. John Kee always talking about a land of opportunity." She looked amused. "Muñoz working for two fifty an hour and hustling skirts to forget. They all just going along with the system, making it more difficult for the ones really trying." She shrugged. "At least the old man understood."

"Are you trying, Cecile? I never noticed."

"You never noticed because you only see me here. You never see me at meetings or distributing leaflets or selling newspapers. There are a lot more hours in the day than what I spend in this place."

Margaret looked at her steadily. "Then why do you come?"

"Reasons." She avoided Margaret's eyes. "You wouldn't understand."

"I'd like to try."

Cecile took out a handkerchief and wiped it across her forehead and under her neck. It gave her an extra few seconds.

"What I do outside gets intense and sometimes I need a place to come to think. There's a lot of talk going down in the meetings. Coming here helps, that's all."

Margaret thought about it for a minute. "Well, don't let them know you're unsure."

Cecile turned on her. "Who said I'm unsure? I'm one of their best workers and I believe in what we're doing." She raised her voice. "This country is choking itself on capitalism and anything I can do to change that I will. Just passing out notices is not enough. Sometimes you have to act and break laws, and if that's what's asked of me, I won't let them down. Unsure? No way!" She stopped suddenly and looked down at the ground. When next she spoke, it was in a softer tone. "I'm serious, Margaret. I've thought a lot about it. When you're poor and black you grow up real quick." She took a breath. "Anyway, it has nothing to do with anything here. Maybe we should get back to work. All this talk's not pulling any weeds."

"I had no idea . . ."

"Well, now you do. Let's drop it."

"If you want," Margaret said politely and glanced down at the bottle of insecticide still in her hand. "About this stuff . . ."

"What about it?" Cecile pulled up suddenly.

"I guess we can do without it. At least for now."

A tiny smile crossed Cecile's face "You know, I bet you never even had anything organic."

"Can't say. I never read labels."

"Labels! Damn! I'm going to make you some of my special corn bread. Then you'll see."

"Is it good?"

"Good? Ain't nothing can touch it."

"Thanks," Margaret said and bent down slowly. She rested on her knees in the soft earth. "I'd like that."

They worked in silence for a few minutes, neither one looking at the other. Vinnie's radio was the only sound in the garden. Finally Cecile interrupted.

"Typical. Robbing an old guy like that. Never had much money. Gonna rob someone, should hit the fat cats." She yanked a stubborn weed out. "Typical!"

In fifteen minutes the row was clean of weeds. Margaret moved over to the dahlias and spent another forty-five minutes carefully tending the delicate plants. After weeding, she thinned out the leaves of nearby plants to make sure her pet flowers would get the right amount of sun. When she was finished, it was close to lunchtime. She glanced at her watch and called over to Cecile.

"Stop for lunch?"

"No," Cecile said. "I'll work straight through." She pointed over to the corn. "Ask Vinnie." Margaret nodded and followed the sound of the radio. She walked along one of the walls, past the cucumbers, and found him on his knees busily grooming the soil between the corn plants.

"Lunchtime," she said. "You bring anything?"

"Two dollars." The mirrored sunglasses still hid his eyes, but his mouth formed into a tight grin.

"Good. We can go together." The idea seemed to please him. He got up, hung the radio over one shoulder, and followed her out. In five minutes they were seated in one of the booths of a coffee shop on Broadway. The radio was up on the table, looking like the instrument panel of some modern sports car. A low syncopated disco rhythm was coming from its dual speakers. Vinnie followed along on the Formica top with a knife, too absorbed in the beat to notice the waitress.

"What do you want to eat?" Margaret asked.

"Cheeseburger. Lots of onions." He kept tapping on the table.

"Make it two," Margaret said to the waitress, "and I'll have tea." She sat back in the seat and looked across at Vinnie. Even with his glasses on, he gave off a definite impression that made Margaret uncomfortable. His face was marked by a few scars from recent blemishes, and his nose made a subtle change of direction somewhere near the bridge. It was hard to tell his age from his face, but his clothes, a style Margaret thought was called "punk," indicated a certain youthfulness. A recent touch Margaret noticed, a tiny safety pin hanging from one of his ears, did not make her feel any more at ease.

His tapping continued.

"Did you know about Luiz?" Margaret asked right away. "About what happened?" The knife stopped in midair as the beat from the radio continued.

"Something happen to Luiz?"

Margaret nodded. "I thought you knew. He had an accident. He's . . ." She hesitated and watched him. "He's dead."

The knife came down again and took up the beat. After a full half minute he said, "No kidding?"

"I thought maybe some of the others would have mentioned it."

He shook his head silently. "Nobody said nothing."

"It was during a robbery. He must have resisted."

"Bad to resist," Vinnie said. "Get hurt that way." Then for the first time it seemed to register. "It's too bad. Luiz was okay." He stopped tapping and put the knife down. Then in a movement that surprised Margaret, he reached over and turned the radio off.

"Were you friendly with him, Vinnie? I never really saw the two of you talk much."

"We did," Vinnie said, "especially back up on 111th Street."

"You knew him from before?"

"Yeah. He'd come by most of the time to watch our stickball games. Me and The Stallions had a standing offer. We take on any six guys for twenty dollars. Just for kicks."

"And he'd watch?"

"Yeah, and sometimes umpire. Things got pretty hot. My friend Sal once cut a guy for being tripped around second. Would have been the winning run." He gestured with his hand and Margaret frowned at the ugly red welt on his wrist.

"What's that?" She nodded.

Immediately Vinnie put his hand down.

"Just a burn."

"Is it painful?"

"Nah." He rolled his hand over and exposed the disfigured blotch of skin. "Happened a coupla years ago."

"It looks like it's from cooking, hot grease or something." Margaret shook her head in sympathy.

Vinnie looked out the window for a second.

"It was a butane lighter."

Margaret's eyes widened. "Someone held you?"

"No," he said calmly. "I did it." He took a sip of water and pulled his hand back. "They didn't think I would. So I showed them. Thought I was some punk kid."

"Who?"

"The Stallions—guys up on 111th. Then they let me join them." He sat back, expressionless, as though what he'd said was old gossip. "Here's the burger. You want your pickle?"

She shook her head and watched as he bit into his food. It was another minute before he looked up again.

"Yeah, I knew Luiz. So what?"

Margaret started in on her own cheeseburger. She was halfway through it before she answered him.

"I heard, Vincent, that you had been in some trouble with the police."

He stopped eating and looked down dully at his plate.

"That's old stuff. I was a kid then."

"What happened?"

He shrugged. "Just out looking for kicks, that's all. I was dumb."

"You call a mugging kicks?"

His forehead creased and she realized his eyes had narrowed. "How'd you know?"

"It doesn't matter, Vincent." There was a silence while he looked at her. "Vincent, would you mind taking off your glasses," she said finally, trying to sound polite. "At my age I don't need mirrors."

He slowly reached up and took off the glasses. The eyes behind them were as impenetrable as the reflecting surfaces.

"You think I'm mixed up with Luiz's death?" His voice was raised. She put her hand on his arm.

"I'm not accusing you of anything. Luiz was a friend and I'm trying to understand what happened."

Vincent reached out and turned on the radio. Immediately loud music filled the corner of the coffee shop. He adjusted the volume and brought it back down.

"I ain't involved," he said simply and picked up his knife again. "We got on good. Whyn'tcha ask some of the others. Ask Jerry."

"Why Jerry?"

Vincent smiled slowly. " 'Cause Jerry'd do anything for a dollar."

"I've spoken to him," she said. "I don't think he'd go that far."

"Oh, no?" Vinnie raised his voice over the radio. "Then he didn't tell you about the fight he had with Luiz?"

"Jerry never mentioned anything about a fight." Margaret frowned.

"No, he wouldn't. Neither would Luiz. But it happened. One night late in the garden after everyone left. I was just leaving when I heard Luiz raise his voice, so I came back and listened. They almost came to blows."

"When was that?" Margaret reached for a cigarette.

He sounded reluctant to continue. "Two days before Luiz disappeared."

She lit it and inhaled deeply. "What did they argue about?"

He raised the volume on his radio again in a gesture of finality.

"Ask Jerry."

"You won't tell me?"

He shook his head slowly. "I've said enough. Rattin' on somebody was never cool. Guys on 111th found out I could do something like that they'd never speak to me again."

"This isn't 111th Street," Margaret said brusquely. "We're talking about murder."

"People gettin' murdered all the time." He shrugged. "Unh-unh. Leave me out of it." He reached into his pocket and put two dollars on the table. "I've said enough." He got up. "You coming?"

She looked at him steadily for a minute, trying to pierce his blank expression.

"No, you go ahead."

"I'd wait," he said, "but there's work to do."

"I understand," she said, finishing off her tea. "I have things to do myself."

25

FORTUNATELY she had her New York Public Library card with her. After leaving the restaurant, she made a quick detour to the nearest branch and spent five minutes talking to the librarian. The two of them then fumbled together through one area of the stacks until Margaret found the medical book she was looking for. It didn't take her long to read the entire article. There were no interruptions and in an hour she closed the book and sat back. Interesting, she thought. Then she left the library and walked home.

The phone was ringing as she entered the door. Schaeffer's voice came through almost before she had the receiver to her ear.

"Anything yet?"

"That's a fine way to say hello."

"Sorry, Margaret. . . . Hello." He took a breath. "Now, what've you got?"

"I just came back from a pleasant morning with two of my coworkers, that's all. Don't be so impatient."

"It's not me who's impatient, it's Morley. He's on my back night and day on this thing. I gotta give him something. You just can't stick a quarter of a million dollars down a hole and turn your back on it."

"Yes, you can. Because if you stand around watching, nothing will happen. I'm surprised at you, David. I'm doing the best I can. I'm sorry, but I don't have anything definite yet."

"I'm sorry too, because Morley's not going to like it. He's already threatening to pull the stones out."

"He wouldn't do that!" There was a silence. "He gave me his word."

"For a quarter of a million and maybe his job he can break it. You really don't have anything? It's over a week." There was silence on the phone while Margaret tried to decide.

"All right. Tell him I've narrowed it down to two of them. I need more time and some questions answered before I can go further. And, if it makes him feel any better, as of last night the stones were still there."

"Still there? How do you know?" He sounded surprised.

"Because while you were watching Ingrid Bergman and Claude Rains, I was on my knees checking. I don't want to lose them either."

"I thought you went to bed early last night."

She chuckled. "David, sometimes I can't keep my days straight. It must have been the night before."

"You old faker," he said. There was a pause. "How'd you narrow it down to two?"

"I can't tell you yet. Morley gave me two weeks, and that means another six days. Just tell him he gave me his word. I promise that as soon as I know anything I'll call."

"And that's it?"

"That's it. Now I've got some other things to do today, so if there's no more—"

"Hold it." Schaeffer now sounded impatient. "Yes

there's more. I want to know how the kids are taking it. What they think of your questioning them.''

"Curious at first. Then mostly helpful. No one's threatened me if that's what you're asking. I've made sure not to mention anything about the diamonds.''

"No one's told you to mind your own business?''

"David,'' she sighed. "You worry too much. There's a good Preston Sturges on tonight. You should watch it, it might relax you some.'' She heard him say something emphatic into the phone, then the line went dead. She stared at it for a brief moment, then put her own receiver on its cradle.

"Imagine that,'' she said. "I've never heard him curse before.''

26

"I never thought I'd see you in here twice," Jerry said. He was just straightening up from a two wall side pocket shot, sinking the five ball off the nine. "Fact is I was just on my way over to the garden. No one left around here to play with." Margaret looked around at the dozen or so other shooters at nearby tables and raised an eyebrow. "I mean for money. They're just rookies."

"I thought your game was Ping-Pong?"

"Either one." He shrugged. "Having two broadens the market. AT & T is into lasers, right? Here"—he reached over to the wall—"grab a stick. Long as you're here you might as well have a little fun."

"No, Jerry. I came to ask you something. I never—"

"Come on, I'll show you." He racked the balls, then broke them. When they came to rest, the cue ball was lined up directly on the number four sitting in front of the end pocket. He smiled.

"Your shot."

"I mean, Jerry. This is ridiculous. I don't even know how to hold this thing."

"Put your hand like this, hold it here. Take a few practice shots. That's it." He walked over behind her. "Now get down low and aim the stick for the center of that white ball. Slow and easy . . . right." She heard the two balls as they clicked together and just saw the number four as it rolled over the edge and toppled into the pocket. When she straightened up, there was a broad grin on her face. She looked behind her.

"Next ball?"

"Try the three. That's your best shot."

"Which one's the three?" She looked over the table. "I can't see the number."

"The one by the side pocket. Just tap it lightly."

"When do I put on the chalk? I once saw that in an Edward G. Robinson movie."

He laughed. "Just take the shot."

This time she missed. "Do I get another chance?"

"Not yet. Wait until I miss." Margaret waited through two racks before she politely walked over to the wall and put her cue back.

"I know when I'm beaten. Now can we talk?"

"Go ahead. Don't mind me. I want to practice a few shots."

She pulled a stool over and sat down. In a minute she had a cigarette lit. "Jerry, what did you argue with Luiz about?"

He didn't miss a beat. He was in the middle of a shot and the cue ran smoothly through his fingers. He didn't even look up. He waited until the white ball came to a stop, then aimed again.

"Who told you we had an argument? Someone bug the zucchini?"

"Vincent. Was he making it up?"

"No." The cue ball cracked into the number one and sent

it caroming across the table. At the end of its run it rolled lazily into an end pocket. "No, we argued." He stood up and looked at Margaret. "But I can't tell you what about. It's private." He winked. "Fifth Amendment."

She inhaled on the cigarette and frowned. "Jerry, Luiz was killed two nights later. What I'm asking is important."

"I'm sure it is," he said. "But it's still private. If Vincent overheard us, ask him. He's got a mouth."

Jerry bent over the table again. "A big one. Besides, it has nothing to do with Luiz's death, I promise you. It's all very innocent."

"If it was so innocent, what were you doing in the garden a week later at midnight?" This time Margaret sounded angry. "What's going on, Jerry? Tell me. I can assure you the police won't be as understanding."

He missed the shot completely and sank the eight ball.

"The police?" He looked at her and all of a sudden his face lost its casual indifference. A new and frightened look took over. "What do they have to do with it?"

"They're looking for Luiz's murderer. It's that simple."

"Well, it wasn't me, I swear." He put his cue back on the table and took a step away. "You gotta believe me. All that other stuff has nothing to do with it."

"So, then you were there at midnight?"

"Yes."

"What were you digging for?"

His eyes turned round and questioning. "How did—"

"Never mind that. What were you digging for when everyone else in their right mind was asleep?"

"I wasn't digging for anything. I was . . ." He stopped.

She got down off the stool and took a step closer. "Yes?"

"I was taking some plants out, that's all. Now cut it out. I didn't kill Luiz. He was my friend. I haven't done a thing." He started to back away.

"And the argument . . ." Margaret began to say but in

the next moment Jerry turned and hurried toward the door. He brushed into one of the other patrons awkwardly, then disappeared down the staircase. Margaret stared in his direction for a few moments, slowly shaking her head. She didn't notice one of the spectators from a nearby table detach himself and glide over. He was in his forties and looked like he'd spent all his life indoors. He came slowly around the table and stood next to her.

"Pardon me," he said smoothly.

"Yes?" Margaret turned her head.

"I couldn't help noticing how good a shooter you are. Care to have a friendly game?" He smiled and his mustache rose at one end.

"Who do you think you're kidding, mister," she said, and walked quickly to the exit.

27

THE next morning, bright and early, Margaret found Bertie on her favorite bench. Sid was sitting nearby reading a copy of *The Wall Street Journal*. He was dressed in his plaid Bermuda shorts and cabby's hat. Could only mean one thing, she thought. A good day yesterday at Aqueduct. She wiped off the bench with a handkerchief and sat down next to Bertie.

"How are they?" She pointed to the birds.

"Hungry as ever." Bertie shifted closer to her friend and lowered her voice. "Where've you been? I missed you yesterday."

"Working in the garden. Asking questions. Keeping an eye on things. Nothing yet to report."

Bertie looked disappointed. "I thought surely there'd be something."

Margaret shook her head. "No, not yet. But soon, I promise. I'm about to start getting tough."

Bertie drew even closer. "How?"

"I haven't quite thought it out yet." Out of the corner of her eye she saw Sid fold his paper and slide the few feet over to them.

"Hello, Margaret. Bertie tell you about my big score yesterday?"

"No, I'm afraid we weren't talking about you, Sid." She saw his face drop momentarily. "What kind of score?" she recovered.

"Oh, just some foolish horse again," Bertie piped up. "He's always losing his money, so the one time he wins, we all gotta suffer."

"Hundred and ninety dollars," Sid said with a big grin.

"Congratulations."

He sat back satisfied. "At least someone appreciates my skill."

"Humph," Bertie snorted. "Just luck if you ask me."

"Luck!" He rolled his eyes. "No such thing as luck in this world. Just hard work and ability. You see the way I study those sheets. Isn't that right, Margaret?"

She shrugged as if the question were beyond her.

"I mean, take your garden," he pressed. "It's not luck that all those plants are coming up so nice. Lotta hard work went into that."

"That's true." She smiled.

"And without it you wouldn't have had nearly as nice vegetables or pretty flowers."

She leaned closer, warming to the subject. "Have you seen the dahlias, Sid?"

"What dahlias?"

They both looked at him. Margaret's smile widened.

"When were you there last?"

"This morning. On my way here I passed by."

"And you didn't see the dahlias?" Bertie asked. "Yesterday they must have been two feet high. Could see them plain from the street."

"Only flowers I saw were some yellow things around the edge and a rose or two up front."

"What!" Margaret jumped up. "You're kidding."

Sid turned red. "Damn it, Margaret. I know what a dahlia looks like. They were my wife Emma's favorite flower. If there'd been any there I'da known."

She looked at him and frowned. "Something's happened." She grabbed her handbag and rushed across the street. Bertie trotted after her.

"Women!" Sid said, shook his head, and went back to reading the paper. "Never understand them. More excited over a bunch of flowers than over a long-shot double."

The bus took only eight minutes to make it to 102nd Street. It took Margaret and Bertie another three to go the rest of the way to the garden. Margaret had a terrible premonition. She fumbled in her handbag for the key, but even before she found it, she knew. In the space between the two rows where the flowers should have been there was only emptiness. The two women rushed in.

"What happened?" Bertie was aghast. Now that they were closer, Margaret could see clearly. The stems were still there, but the flowers had been snipped an inch below the bud. They lay like a rank of decapitated heads at the base of each stalk, muddy and limp in the morning sun. Margaret looked quickly around but as far as she could tell, nothing else had been touched. Just the dahlias, and that she knew held a special message. They were her flowers.

"I've scared someone," she said. "It's a warning." She bent and picked up one of the closest heads, a shimmery purple with a fringe of lavender. "Pity they had to take it out on the flowers." She carefully wrapped it in a Kleenex and put it in her bag.

"Gives me the shivers," Bertie said, looking at the row of ruined flowers. "It's perverse, that's what it is."

"Well, whatever else it may be," Margaret said, "it was stupid. Whoever did it took a big risk."

"How?"

"Because it quite clearly establishes that I've been on the right track all along." Margaret turned to Bertie. "So, whoever did it thinks I frighten easily."

"What will you do?"

"What they want. I won't ask any more questions."

"No?"

Margaret shook her head. "It's past that now. Now's the time for action. It's time I applied some pressure. I've got five days. I think that will be long enough."

"For what?"

Margaret smiled. "Bertie, do you have an old blanket?"

Her friend gave her a puzzled look.

"I was thinking it might be nice to have a picnic in the country later on this afternoon."

28

MORLEY looked down angrily at the hot pastrami sandwich in front of him. It was a few hours later and the two policemen were having an early lunch. He picked it up and glanced across the desk.

"She was upset because her goddamn dahlias were cut? Is she serious?"

Schaeffer nodded. "It's what she said over the phone. But she wanted you to know that she's not worried."

"Well, Christ, she should be." Morley bit down on his sandwich too hard and some of the mustard squirted out onto the paper. "I don't like it," he continued. "Someone's made it very clear they don't want her around and the next time they won't be so polite. She ought to pull out."

"Look, Sam, I understand your problem. I know your ass is on the line if it goes wrong, especially if something happens to Margaret."

"It's not my ass I'm worried about, damn it; it's hers."

"Figure it this way. Someone took the trouble to threaten her, so she was right. It's one of those five kids."

"You think I care?" Morley exploded. "You really think I would trade off putting another punk kid away if it meant risking her? I think we're crazy going this far with it."

Schaeffer took a moment to finish off his cream soda. "Doesn't sound like the old you."

"It's not." He got up and paced to the window. "This time's different. Maybe I'm getting older, but it doesn't seem as important."

Schaeffer shrugged and there was silence in the small office for a minute. The typewriters from the next room sounded very near. "So what do you want me to do?" he asked shortly. "You know she won't volunteer to quit."

Morley stared out the window, thinking of the last time they had tried to force her hand. "Yeah, that won't work. She's like a little terrier, especially when it has to do with one of her friends. You can't talk sense, you can't threaten." He looked on the desk for his cigarettes. "Only thing you can do is lock her up . . . or hope she's smart enough to stay out of trouble. But this time . . ."

"We could just dig up the stones without her knowing," Schaeffer said.

Morley considered that for a moment. "No good. We might have gotten away with that before she started, but not now. If the thief checks on the stones and finds them missing, Margaret's the first one he'll go after. No, the stones have to stay until he's caught or we convince Margaret to forget the whole thing and take a vacation."

"Little chance of that."

"Yeah." Morley looked disgusted. "We got ourselves into a real trap this time."

"So you'll let her continue?" Schaeffer leaned back slowly.

"She said she narrowed it down to two?"

"That's what she said."

"Did she say which ones?"

"Not even a hint. What I really think"—Schaeffer leaned forward—"is that she doesn't want us entering into her investigation. She's playing it real close."

"Too close," Morley said angrily. "One day she's gonna get jammed." There was a pause while Morley lit a cigarette.

"I'll tell her then she has your blessing?"

"No, just tell her she's got five days." Morley sat back down. "After that you can tell her we'll be out of the diamond business. And, Dave . . ." He looked up and there was a kind of understanding that passed between them. "Keep an eye on her."

"Don't worry," Schaeffer said. "Like she was my own mom."

29

"YOU never fail to amaze me," Bertie said. "I never thought he'd do it." The two ladies were standing near the Hertz rental counter, nervously watching as Sid made the arrangements to get a car for the afternoon.

"Well, he's the only one with a license," Margaret whispered. "They won't rent you a car without one."

"What'd you tell him?"

"I promised to go to the track with him one day." Margaret smiled. "You know how he is about that."

Bertie chuckled. "You weren't serious."

"Oh, yes. In fact I told him you'd come too. It was the least I could do."

Bertie gave her friend a scornful look. In another minute Sid walked over and quietly motioned them to the sidewalk, out of view of the counter.

"This is crazy," he said, "but here it is." He handed Margaret the keys and all the paperwork. "You're sure you know how to drive?"

"I told you, Oscar and I used to drive up through New Jersey to the Catskills every summer. Sure I know how to drive. I just haven't bothered renewing my license for a while." She stuffed the papers into her handbag. "Which one is it?"

"It's the red Cougar." Sid pointed to the ramp. They walked over and Margaret got in the driver's side. Bertie came around and sat next to her. Sid stuck his head through the window and pointed out the controls. When he was finished, Margaret still had a puzzled look on her face.

"What's the matter?"

"Where's the choke?"

"Choke! When's the last time you drove?" he said.

"Nineteen forty-eight. Don't worry, I'll manage. It's like riding a bicycle. You never forget." Sid and Bertie exchanged nervous glances before he took a step back and Margaret started the engine. It roared to life and a pleased grin spread across her face. "There now," she said. "I told you I knew how to drive. 'Bye, Sid, see you tomorrow." She shifted into drive and stepped on the gas. Tires squealed for twenty yards and she just managed to make the turn at the end of the ramp. She slowed down and eased herself into traffic on Eleventh Avenue.

"Where are we going?" Bertie asked anxiously. Her hand was locked onto the armrest.

"First to buy some picnic food. Then to my apartment for some empty boxes. Then"—Margaret turned sideways and smiled—"to New Jersey."

They drove for an hour and a half before they neared their destination. Margaret had trouble making left turns across traffic and preferred making three rights and going around an entire block instead. The superhighways frightened her so she stayed in the right lane and kept her speed to a comfortable thirty-five. Bertie kept checking the road map and finally she looked up and pointed.

"This is it. Wanaque Reservoir, Ringwood Manor State Park. Turn here."

Margaret slammed on the brakes and all the food tumbled off the seat, but she managed to steer the car off the highway. Horns blared in anger as cars behind her narrowly missed her back end.

"We should do this more often," Margaret said. "It's nice to get out of the city once in a while. How much farther on this road?"

"Only a few miles. We're almost there." They drove on, chatting gaily about the trees and birds they saw outside the windows. They were passing through hilly, forested terrain with few commercial roadside spots and Margaret couldn't help thinking back to the drives she'd taken with Oscar. The empty boxes in the trunk were the last thing on her mind.

"Here we are," Bertie said. "How'd you ever think of this place?"

"I looked at a map," Margaret said. "If we're going to have a picnic, why not have one in a pretty spot." She looked at her watch. "And it's just the right time too. I'm starved." She drove into the park and continued until the road curved near the calm water of the reservoir. Only a few ducks broke its glassy surface. When she found an open area, she pulled the car off to the side.

"Now, let's see what kind of chef you are. Did we bring the potato chips?"

Bertie got out of the car with the bag of groceries. "Taco chips," she corrected. "Yes, we brought the Taco chips."

Bertie was obviously still miffed at that purchase.

"Well, how about under that tree?" Margaret said, and the two women set off across the small clearing. Margaret spread the blanket and in ten minutes the food was laid out on paper plates. Besides the chips there was cold chicken, coleslaw, and a green salad. They ate slowly, enjoying the spot and the privacy. Margaret talked about her trips with Oscar and about some of the small hotels they had spent pleasant summer nights in. Bertie had been to New Jersey with her husband Tony when he was still alive, but only the southern part near the beach around Atlantic City. "Before the gambling," she said. "Thank God or we'd a been broke long before 1959." Together they reminisced about times when superhighways were still on planning tables and cars without running boards and chokes were oddities.

Finally Margaret looked at her watch and frowned. "It's getting late." She stood up. "I won't be but a few minutes. I want to get some plants to take back. Just relax until I return." She strode off in the direction of the car and the few empty boxes. Bertie sighed, brushed some crumbs off her dress, and leaned back. In a few minutes her eyes were closed.

She woke to the sound of the car trunk being closed. In a minute her friend was by her side. Other than the few dirt spots on her dress and the pair of rubber gloves she was holding, there was no indication that Margaret had spent the last hour digging plants.

"All set?" Bertie asked and yawned.

"I think so. Let's not forget that nursery on the way to the highway. I'm sure they'd have something nice to replace the dahlia row. It's such an eyesore now. Maybe pachysandra. If we hurry we should make it." Bertie struggled up and helped Margaret with the blanket.

"Did you see how nice the water was?" Margaret asked, getting into the car. Bertie smiled.

"Yes, and not a boat or person on it. Kind of different from Broadway. I must admit I wish my birds were with me. The fresh air would do 'em good."

"Come on. I want to get back before dark. I can't remember where Sid said the lights were."

"By the ashtray, I think," Bertie said.

Margaret pulled on a knob and the wipers started moving. "Never mind," she said. "I'll just go a little faster."

Bertie closed the door reluctantly, leaned back in her seat, and stared straight ahead. "Okay," she said, "I'm ready."

After the stop at the nursery they got lost twice on the way back to the city. By the time they pulled up in front of the garden on 102nd Street, it was already dark. The two women slowly got out of the car and took a moment to uncramp their muscles.

"I told you I'd get you home," Margaret said. Bertie mumbled something incomprehensible, moved to the back door, and opened it. She began withdrawing the boxes of pachysandra and placed them by the fence. Margaret opened the trunk and took out the other two boxes from the reservoir. Together they deposited everything in a corner of the garden. In fifteen minutes they were done, the gate locked, and they were back inside the car. A damp, earthy smell still clung to the fabric of the interior. Bertie heaved one tremendous sigh and leaned back. "A very nice afternoon," she said. "But what's it got to do with diamonds?"

"You'll see." Margaret chuckled to herself. "Things should begin to get interesting now."

"Maybe, but all I can think of now is a hot cup of tea and a bath."

"Right away." Margaret stepped on the gas, clipped the fender of the parked car ahead of her, and headed south. "I'll never understand it," she said to herself after a minute. "People parking so far out into the street!"

30

By 5:00 P.M. the next day she was almost finished planting the new row. She worked slowly, careful not to damage the new plants she had brought. Occasionally she looked up at the gate but no one was expected quite yet. She had placed a notice early in the morning, requesting that all the workers try and come that evening around 5:30.

She uprooted the dead dahlias one by one and then slowly put down the hearty-rooted pachysandra. She was just starting on the space between the cucumbers, planting the two boxes of wild plants she had collected, when Cecile appeared. Shortly thereafter the others came in and by 5:30 they were all there, even Jerry.

They were angry when they saw the dahlias, but not everyone was shocked at the apparent meaninglessness of the act. Cecile blamed it on a capitalist conspiracy to block a community effort.

"Bunch of florists probably did it," she snorted. "Anything to keep their prices up."

Vinnie thought it might have been one of the local gangs from uptown. "Maybe the Sabres," he sneered. "We just whipped them last week in stickball."

But Margaret stopped the speculation. "Of all the things in the garden, I worked hardest on the dahlias," she began, her voice steady. "It was a very nasty act. I don't know if it was one of you or someone from the outside."

"One of us a floracidal maniac?" Jerry said in surprise. "Why would any of us do a thing like that? Doesn't make sense."

"It made sense to someone," Margaret said quickly, "and now there are no dahlias."

"Yeah, it's too bad," Peter said. "First ones I ever seen."

There was an uneasy silence for a moment as they all looked where the flowers had been.

"Anyway," Margaret continued, "I couldn't leave the row empty, so I'm filling it with something else." She gestured. "A low creeper with long roots. It should flower in a month and keep the weeds down. This time I'd like to ask that no one come near it. I'm sick about the dahlias and I'd hate to have anything spoil this new row." She waited until they all nodded. "Vandalism is a nasty business; I hope this is the end of it."

"Sure, Margaret," John Kee said sincerely. "We'll be careful." Jerry cleared his throat. "What about the other things? Some of them will be ready soon, the tomatoes and the squash. We should start picking them in a few days."

"Yes," Margaret agreed. "Just please stay away from the pachysandra. As the vegetables ripen we'll pick them together. I'm sorry this awful thing had to happen. I want to forget about it as soon as I can."

"I know it's not much," Cecile said, slightly embarrassed, "but how about that corn bread I told you about—fresh baked."

Margaret shrugged. "You don't have to, Cecile."

"But I want to. Maybe it'll make you feel better."

"Thank you," Margaret said and took a minute to look over the garden. "I suppose the tomatoes should be picked soon. Maybe Wednesday evening." She smiled for the first time. "By then they should be ready."

"It's too bad Luiz can't be here to see it," Vinnie said gloomily. He turned to the others. "It was all his idea."

"Maybe we can do something," John Kee said, "to remember him by."

"Like what?" Muñoz asked.

"I don't know." John Kee thought for a minute. "Maybe we can sell some extra produce and donate it to charity in his name."

"No, I have a better idea," Margaret added quickly. "Something I thought about last night. We should plant something in his name. Something that will last." She looked at them slowly. "I was thinking about a tree."

"A tree," Cecile said and a broad grin crossed her face. "Hey, that's great."

"Yeah," Muñoz added. "A tree for the man would be nice."

"And we can buy it with the money from the vegetables," Margaret continued. "How about it?"

"Sure," Jerry said. "He woulda liked that."

"All right," Margaret said. "I'll take care of everything. Maybe I can arrange it by Wednesday." She bent down and picked up her trowel. "See you all then." She moved off slowly to finish her planting.

Everyone except Jerry turned to go. He hesitated and then came over next to her.

"Can I help?"

"No," Margaret said simply. "I'd rather do this alone." He didn't move and she looked at him questioningly. He picked up a little pebble and worked it around awkwardly in the palm of his hand.

"About the other day," he continued. "Sorry I rushed out like that. You surprised me. I didn't expect anyone would find out."

"No, what else do people grow alongside corn? I suspected right away." She smiled thinly.

"And you won't tell?"

Margaret kept planting. "There's no reason to. It's over with now, right?"

"Yes," Jerry said and dropped the pebble back onto the ground. "I was taking them out that night. It's too bad. Came all the way from Maui."

"What did you do with them?"

He stood up and turned to go. "Oh, they're around." He smiled. "Lotta parks in the city."

He walked away while Margaret continued to prepare the soil for her plants.

"Maui indeed," she said to herself and shook her head in disapproval.

31

THE delivery truck with the tree arrived Wednesday afternoon and Margaret was waiting for it. The neat row of pachysandra was all planted and doing well. The space in the cucumbers was also filled in with the wild plants, except there was one small unplanted area a foot in diameter directly over the box of diamonds. She could imagine the anxiety the empty space caused to the person who knew what was buried underneath.

The two men in the truck brought the tree inside and placed it against one of the walls. Margaret signed the receipt, then turned to look at their new purchase. She had asked for a birch and this was one of the prettiest she'd ever seen. It was still small, only nine feet, but it had the whitest bark and several branches of healthy green serrated leaves. Luiz would have been pleased with it, she mused, running her fingers over the trunk. She gave it a little push but the large burlap ball of roots held it solidly upright. And heavy too . . . good. She gave it one last look and turned to wait for the others.

They all started arriving around 5:30, ready to start harvesting. John Kee brought a large wicker basket that looked like it could hold a bushel of vegetables. Vinnie had a cardboard box with him as well as the radio and Jerry brought a shopping bag from Bonwit Teller. Cecile's bag looked African to Margaret, one of those fiber things she'd seen pictures of in a magazine. It had colorful rings going around the outside of a ball shape and a band that went over her shoulder. As she approached, she had her hand down inside the large bag and was reaching for something Margaret could not see.

"I brought it," the girl said. She pulled out her hand and Margaret caught a glimpse of something metallic.

"What?"

"The corn bread." Cecile smiled. "I wrapped it in foil so it will stay fresh. I made it special, extra spices and things." She handed it to Margaret. "Go ahead, take it."

"Oh, I forgot." Margaret looked around. "Thank you, Cecile. I'll put it over by the lockers for now—out of the way." She took the half dozen steps over, set the bundle down by the wall, and came back. "I'll have some tonight. Now, as soon as Peter gets here, we can all begin." Almost on cue they heard the gate open and Peter came up. His harvest container consisted of a large plastic bag from Crazy Eddie. His tight-fitting, tailored clothes looked out of place next to everyone else's jeans and work clothes.

Margaret motioned everyone over.

"Here it is." She pointed at the birch. "Luiz's memorial tree. Long after the flowers and vegetables are gone this winter we'll still have this to remind us of him. I ordered a plaque but it won't be ready for two days. I thought we could all get together Friday evening, plant the tree, and mount the plaque somehow."

"We'll need some wire and stakes," John Kee said. "And something solid for the plaque. I can get that stuff at school."

"Good." Margaret smiled.

"Where's it going?" Cecile asked.

"In the cucumbers," Margaret said simply. "In that open area I left. Next year we'll build a little pathway to it with borders of flowers, rearrange things a bit. The important thing is to get it into the ground. I'm sure you'll all agree."

There was a slight hesitation.

"I don't think it should go in the middle of the vegetables," Cecile said, frowning. "It's not right for the tree and it's not good for the cucumbers. Why can't we pull up some of the marigolds and plant it there?"

Margaret took a quick breath.

"What, by the wall?" Peter Muñoz said. "No one'd ever see it. Right out in the middle is where we want it, where Margaret said. Besides, the cucumbers are looking pretty healthy. It can't hurt them."

"And no one's pulling out any more flowers," Margaret added decisively. "We've had enough of that."

"Yeah, and the spot's all set," Muñoz said. "What's the hassle?"

Cecile shrugged. "No hassle. I can give an opinion, can't I?" She turned angrily to the side and picked up her bag.

"Okay. Friday then," Margaret said and picked up her own small harvest bag. "We ready?"

"All set," Vinnie said looking over the garden. "Where do we begin?"

"There are tomatoes, zucchini, and some turnips ready . . . and I noticed a few heads of lettuce," Margaret said. "Nothing's ready in the back so there's no need to go there at all. And remember, it's better letting things ripen on the vine than in the kitchen."

They spread out in the front half of the garden and began picking. There was a lot of chattering going on. At one point Vinnie yelled out when he came across an eighteen-inch yarrow hidden under some large leaves. Everyone came over to admire his find. Jerry discovered a bush of cherry tomatoes that was riper than the rest and pointed it out to John Kee. The sun was still above the roofline and after twenty minutes, some began taking off their jackets and sweaters. Peter Muñoz took off his shirt and hung it up on top of one of the old tool lockers. People disappeared now and then between rows of taller plants and reappeared twenty feet farther away. To pick the turnips you had to go on your knees, so at any one time Margaret couldn't tell who was where. Very often her eyes strayed to the open area in the cucumbers purely by reflex, but no one even came close. Not that she expected to see her criminal, spade in hand, uncovering the diamonds. She was just being cautious. After an hour the sun sank down behind the adjoining building, and with the shadows came a little chill to the air. Margaret noticed it first and went to put on her sweater. Peter got his shirt and walked over to her. His bag was full, the handles just about to pop off.

"Small lettuce you got there," Margaret chided. "It's still a baby."

"Only one left," Peter said. "All the bigger ones were taken." He smiled. "Plenty tomatoes though. Should make up for it." She looked and saw a dozen or so big ripe tomatoes and nodded.

"That and some onions and you'll do okay."

Cecile came up and set her bag down with a sigh. It was smaller than Peter's, but the way she handled it, it seemed even heavier. She had a newspaper covering the top.

"Looks heavy," Margaret said. "What've you got?"

"They love cherry tomatoes at home," the girl said, lifting the paper, and sure enough the top third of the bag was filled with the little red vegetables. Only one or two squash were poking through and the tops of a few turnips.

"Very nice," Margaret said. "Should hold you for a week."

"Two, I think," Cecile said and replaced the paper. She

winked at Margaret. "Or I can always pass them out at some meetings."

Just then Margaret heard a tap on the gate and a "Yoo hoo, Margaret." She recognized the voice and turned to see Bertie. Her friend was taking in the activity in the garden with great interest. Margaret walked the half dozen steps over and let her in.

"What's going on? So much commotion."

"It's our first harvest," Margaret said. "Come take a look."

"Really, how exciting." Bertie followed Margaret cautiously along one wall and when they were still a few steps away from everyone she whispered, "is he here?"

"Who?"

"The murderer."

Margaret turned around quickly. "*Shhh.* Bertie!"

"Sorry, Margaret. Frightens me to know it's one of them."

"Not here," and Margaret looked sternly at her. "You'll spoil everything. . . ."

Just then Vinnie walked by and Margaret stopped him. Her expression softened. "See, Bertie, fresh vegetables, a whole boxful."

"Yeah, and all for free," Vinnie said. "That's the best part."

Bertie leaned over and looked down. "That zucchini's nice, go well in a cheese sauce. Tomatoes are a bit green, don'tcha think? But look at that lettuce." Bertie's eyes lit up. "What kind is it?"

"Bibb," Margaret said and lit a cigarette. "Next week we'll have the romaine."

"I can't wait for the corn," Vinnie said and struggled off with his box to the fence. Margaret turned and was about to say something to Bertie when she saw Jerry heading toward the cucumbers. She walked over quickly and got to him just before he entered the row.

"Where are you going?" she asked and took a puff from her cigarette. Some of the smoke got in her eye and she squinted to clear it.

"Look here," Jerry said and opened his bag. "They didn't leave me too much." Margaret looked down and saw about a half dozen ripe tomatoes, a few turnips and one or two squash. "I was hoping I might pick up a few cucumbers. You never can tell, sometimes there's a few early ones just sitting there waiting to be pickled."

Margaret looked at him silently for a few seconds. Her eye was still tearing. "Jerry," she began. "I checked yesterday and it's too soon. Besides, it's not right. Everyone else stayed away and we should all get the same opportunity." Jerry edged away reluctantly. "Don't you think?"

"I guess so." His face took on a guilty expression. "I was really just looking."

"Next week," Margaret said. "Maybe then."

She turned and walked back to Bertie. Her friend was in animated conversation with John Kee, even gesticulating with her hands.

"No, no! Boiled is the best way," she was saying. "Fried beans—never heard of such a thing."

John Kee had a pained expression on his face.

"You don't understand, they're snow peas, and they're sautéed, in a wok."

"A what?"

"A wok."

"What's a wok?" Bertie looked to Margaret for help.

Margaret shrugged. "I think I saw them at Macy's once. They look something like a hubcap with handles." She turned to the air-conditioning student and frowned. "But surely, John, you didn't pick any of them yet. They're much too small."

"Well, just a handful," he said, looking guilty. "But I promise to take less when we pick them later. I just couldn't wait. Here.'' He reached in and fumbled through the top layer of juicy tomatoes before he found his stash of snow peas. ''See, they're edible.''

Margaret shook her head. ''Got to watch you all like a hawk. You don't need a wok for those, more like a soup ladle. She crushed out the cigarette. He turned to go and in passing gave Bertie a big smile.

''You try them sautéed. You'll like them much better.''

''Go on!'' the older women said. ''Give me heartburn for a week.'' She watched as he walked carefully over the rows of vegetables and made his way out the gate.

''Well, I guess that does it,'' Margaret said. ''They've all gone. Suppose we should be leaving too.''

''Not before you tell me what you've been up to. I see you got all those new plants out.'' Bertie looked at her questioningly. ''What's it all about, Margaret? I'm bursting to know.''

''Not here. Let's go to our bench. I'd feel better talking there.''

''And about time too,'' Bertie said. ''Let me give you a hand with your veggies.''

The two women bent down, lifted the sack, and started for the door. Bertie passed through and Margaret got out her key to lock the gate behind her. She gave the garden one last look before leaving. Something caught her attention out of the corner of her eye.

''Oh, my.'' She stopped. ''I nearly forgot. Be right back.'' She opened the door again, walked over to the side wall, and was back in a minute. ''Fresh corn bread.'' She held it up and smiled. ''Can't wait to try it tonight. Cecile baked it.''

''Corn bread's my favorite,'' Bertie said. ''Used to make it for my Tony once a month. Only on special occasions.''

''Well, then you take some too.''

''No, I couldn't.''

Margaret insisted. "It would take me two weeks to finish it all," and in a jiffy she had the foil open, and the loaf in two halves. She wrapped it up again and handed one of the packages to her friend. "Nice and moist too," Margaret noted. "Come on, let's go before all the seats are taken." The two women once again picked up the bag of produce and trudged with it between them toward Broadway.

32

BERTIE hardly noticed the traffic rushing by them on Broadway as they sat on their little island bench.

"A little birch tree?" She couldn't believe her ears. "You're going to plant a tree!"

"Right in that open spot over the diamonds," Margaret said. "I figure that if anything should get the criminal to move, that will. Besides"—Margaret leaned back—"I thought it would look quite nice in the garden afterwards, so the money wouldn't be wasted at all."

Bertie looked skeptical. "Then what?"

"That's when our friends the police come in. I'm on my way to tell David to keep an eye on the garden. Like before, only this time it's going to work. Don't you see? The criminal may have suspected I was onto something but up to now was always too cautious to move. But with that row of creepers going everywhere except over the treasure, well, that's going to start some anxious thoughts: 'Maybe the old girl doesn't scare off so easily." She chuckled and fingered her half of the corn bread by her side. "Then I play my trump and threaten with the tree, threaten to dig right down to the loot and spoil everything. At that point he's got to move. He can't risk it. Only thing is," she grinned, "we'll be waiting. David will catch him with the diamonds, and that's that." She smiled. "That's what I've been doing. It's really quite simple. Just gotta stay one step ahead all the time."

"And it's one of your kids?" Bertie asked. "One of them in the garden?"

"Oh, yes."

Bertie's eyes opened. "You know which one it is?"

"I think so," Margaret said evenly. "I suspected before, but now I'm pretty sure."

"Well, who?"

Margaret shook her head. "Sorry, Bertie. I can't tell you. Not yet, anyway. I can't risk it right now." She started to get up.

"But Margaret . . ."

"No, Bertie. If I told you, you'd be around tomorrow peering right into the culprit's face, clucking your tongue. You're really not a good actress, you know. This last scene has to be played quite normally. Best to have you not know, then you can't make a mistake." She picked up her half of the corn bread and turned to go.

"But, Margaret," her friend pressed, "what if he's one step ahead of you?" She reddened. "I mean it's a possibility. He's done it once."

"Luiz didn't know." Margaret smiled. "I do. Come by tomorrow. Then you can tell me how you liked Cecile's corn bread."

Bertie nodded absently. "Good-bye, Margaret. Be careful."

"I will," Margaret said.

*   *   *

Schaeffer was in when she arrived at the precinct.

"Can we talk?" Margaret asked. "It's important."

"Sure. Over here." He directed her to an empty side office, pulled out a chair for her, then sat on the desk. "What's the problem, Sherlock?"

"David, I need help. I need you to watch the garden for the next two nights."

Schaeffer scratched his beard and leaned forward. "Why?"

She explained about the tree. "Friday's the deadline. I'm sure the thief will move tonight or tomorrow night," she concluded.

Schaeffer glanced at his watch. "Morley's gone for the day. He's the only one can authorize a full stakeout tonight. I don't know if I can reach him . . ."

"Forget Morley then," she said abruptly. "We don't need his hot dog van. There are plenty of places someone can stand and be out of sight. I was thinking of just you and me."

"Impossible," Schaeffer said and stood up. "I might decide to do it, but there's no way I'm going to let you come along."

"But, David . . ."

"No, 'buts,' Margaret. I promised Morley I'd keep you out of trouble and that does not mean taking you on a stakeout. Besides, I'd have my hands full. Unh-unh." He looked at her for a moment. "Make up your mind."

"Can you do it alone?"

"Sure, I've been up twenty-four hours straight before," Schaeffer said, smiling. "Maybe we'll be lucky this time."

"It could be tomorrow night too," Margaret said, fidgeting.

"Tomorrow we'll tell Morley and if he buys it, he'll give me Jacobson. It's always better with two. . . ."

She looked up.

". . . Cops I mean. But you got to promise me to stay home tonight. Lock the door. Don't let anybody in."

"Sounds like an order."

"It is."

"Well," she sighed and got out of the chair. "Under the circumstances, I promise." She put a hand on Schaeffer's arm. "David, I'm sorry to run you around like this. I realize it's not healthy."

"Occupational hazard," he said and reached for the door. "Meet you tomorrow morning in Morley's office at nine."

"On the dot," she said, walked through the door and out of the station house.

The sun was just setting and the streetlights flickered on, but Bertie didn't notice. She had been sitting on the bench for the last hour, her mind on the five gardeners, trying to figure out which one it could be. She'd seen them all and had her own opinions. But she tried to remember what Margaret had said about each one. There was Peter, that little Romeo. 'Course it could be him, Bertie thought. That type's always getting into trouble. Didn't Margaret say she couldn't understand why he came to the garden, he seemed so out of place. Then that little hustler, what's his name. Jerry. And his brother the diamond setter. That one's a natural. She nodded knowingly to herself. A bus went by and she glanced idly at the advertisement on the side. It was a picture of a new television set and that inspired a new train of thought: The one with the radio—Vinnie. Inconsiderate like all the rest of 'em, playing that loud music even on crowded buses. Wouldn't put it past him. In fact, she thought, wouldn't put it past any of them. Kids these days got nothing better to do than make trouble. Not like in my day. She reached deliberately into her handbag and pulled out her compact, pressed the catch, and looked at her forehead in the mirror. It was always reassuring, her forehead. Hadn't changed too much in the last fifteen years, not like under her chin, where the wrinkles seemed to bunch up like waves in a storm. But she took out the rouge puff anyway and took some of the shine off above her eyebrows. In my day none of this woulda happened. Ten minutes over the old man's knee—best learning there was! She closed the compact and looked up just in time to see Roosa slide somewhat unsteadily onto the bench next to her. Even from two feet away she could smell the balmy ether of Old Grand-dad.

"Evenin', Bertie," the older man said. His face cranked itself up into a formal smile, then dropped just as quickly. "Seen you sitting here all alone. Thought I'd say 'lo."

Bertie nodded and closed her handbag with a resounding snap. Then, like an old hen fluffing out her feathers, she brushed off her sweater with great care and sat back solidly on the bench.

"Don't know why you'd think I'd want to say hello to you when you're in that state. Embarrassing, it is, be seen sitting here with you."

"Come orf it," Roosa said and leaned over toward her. "Seen you myself in worse condition. Don't be so high an' mighty. Ain't no crime now is it?"

"Besides, I was thinking," she added. "Something important on my mind. You interrupted."

"Christ," he said. "Never mind. I'll just lean back and take a nap." With that he set his head on the back of the bench and closed his eyes. Bertie looked at him cautiously for a moment, waiting for him to sit up and revive the conversation. But in two minutes he was snoring. She elbowed him gently.

"Joseph, wake up."

"Huh?"

"I got a problem."

"Atsamatter?" It took another minute before his eyes adjusted. "You still here?"

"Joseph, listen. You think it's possible for a young girl to kill someone? I don't know. It don't sit right with me. Sixteen, seventeen years old. What do you think?" She looked at him for an answer.

" 'Course," he said and rubbed his chin. "Happens alla time. Don't you read the papers?"

"Still an' all," Bertie said half to herself. "I prefer one of the boys. Makes more sense."

"No idea what you're talking about," Roosa said and grinned foolishly. "You planning a murder?"

"Trying to figure one out."

"Oh, I see." He gave a little grunt and shifted back into his nap position. "Must be the weather," he said after a minute and closed his eyes again.

She thought about that for a while, then finally asked, "What's the weather?"

"No pigeons. Usually flocks of 'em birds around when you're here."

"Oh." She looked down and for the first time noticed that he was right. "They only come if I bring them something. They're smart enough not to get excited by nothing."

"Still I thought they were your friends."

"They are." Bertie reddened and gave the older man a cross look, but he was oblivious. She saw his red-veined cheeks moving in and out with his heavy breathing. Trying to get my goat, she thought and looked away. Her eyes fell on Cecile's corn bread.

"Or maybe they're sleepin'," he added. "I wouldn't take it personal."

Damn the man, Bertie thought and lifted the bread. It took her only a split second to make up her mind. She unwrapped the aluminum foil, carefully pulled a section off, and scattered some of it out in front of her. Margaret won't mind. Be nice to give them a treat now and then, she thought. She waited a few minutes in silence until the first pigeons flew up, then gave Roosa a defiant nudge.

"Here they are," she said proudly. "Didn't I tell you?"

With one eye open and the other closed, Roosa reached into his pocket and pulled out a pint bottle of whiskey. He upended it for a good two swallows before he ventured a comment.

"Little buggers!"

One hopped onto the bench next to him and he shooed it off. "All they do is eat and shit, eat and shit—kinda life is that?"

Bertie scattered half the remaining bread and stood up to go. When Joseph got too drunk and started swearing, it was always a bad sign. What usually followed was a long monologue and then a quick fade. She'd seen him pass out in some very awkward places, like the rear of the number 104 bus. Best not to be around when it happened. Besides it was getting late.

"Good night, Joseph," she said frostily. "If I were you I wouldn't drink any more tonight. You know how you get." She picked up her handbag. "One day something awful's gonna happen and don't say I didn't tell you so." On that note she turned impressively and started to walk away. She got five steps before he called out.

"Bertie." She didn't hear him.

"Bertie!"

She stopped and looked back. "Now what?"

"Something awful just happened." He had a wrinkled smile on his face. "I think one of your goddamn birds just died on my right shoe."

33

MARGARET took the lamb chop out of the oven and set it on the table. The creamed spinach was already steaming in its own bowl alongside the little tomato and lettuce salad from the garden. Cecile's corn bread was unwrapped and sitting on a plate with a good-sized square of butter. Everything was ready for a nice quiet dinner.

Margaret sat down lightly and surveyed it all.

"Oh, the flower," she said and got up. By the window was the cut dahlia she had rescued in its own shallow bowl of water. The petals had fanned out so that it looked like a purple water lily. She brought it back to the table. "There, all set." She cut into the lamb chop and chewed it appreciatively. She was thinking what a treat the whole meal was Chops were so expensive these days she could only afford them on special occasions. But she could think of no better time than with her first harvest. She took a tiny crumb of corn bread and put it in her mouth.

Strange spices she uses, Margaret thought and took a sip of

water. Then again, I never did understand health food. All that protein and ginseng root.

She took a spoonful of spinach, then attacked the chop once again. She glanced at the flower and a sadness came over her. She couldn't help thinking about Luiz. Poor man. There was a little comfort in knowing that the person who killed him wouldn't get away. She took another spoon of spinach, then cut off a thick slice of the corn bread and buttered it. She was lifting it to her mouth when the phone rang. Who could that be? she thought and looked at the bread a few inches away. She put it down, walked the few steps, and lifted the receiver.

"Yes?"

There was silence on the other end, the kind of silence that came from someone not talking. It was an alive emptiness.

"Hello, hello, who is it?"

Still nothing. Maybe faint sounds of breathing.

"Sid, is that you with another joke?" She waited a few seconds, then put the receiver back down slowly. She moved to the table with a frown. "Now who . . . ?" She picked up her fork without thinking and stabbed a wedge of tomato, forgetting the slice of bread for the moment. Could be a wrong number I suppose. Impolite not apologizing. Then she realized she was eating one of her own tomatoes and smiled. She tried the lettuce and was just as pleased. In another minute she forgot about the phone call and concentrated on her meal. There was still Cecile's bread to try, buttered and ready, and she lifted it once again. "Nice color," Margaret remarked, and opened her mouth.

The loud knocking at the door startled her. Then the doorknob rattled. "Margaret! Margaret!"

She got up, still holding the bread, and went to the door. "Bertie, is that you?"

"Open up!"

Margaret undid the lock and the door flew open. Her friend

burst in, took one look, and threw her arms around Margaret.

"Thank God you're all right."

"Bertie, what's come over you? Of course I'm all right."

Then Bertie saw the bread in her friend's hand and her eyes narrowed. "You haven't had any yet?" Her voice wavered just the slightest.

Margaret looked down. "Why no, I was just about to when—"

Bertie didn't let her finish. She grabbed the bread out of Margaret's hand and put it back on the table. Then she sat down heavily, put her head in her hands, and started crying.

"What on earth . . . ?"

"They all died," Bertie said through her tears. "I thought I'd be too late."

Margaret sat down gently next to her. "What?"

"The bread. Cecile poisoned the bread. She was going to kill you." She looked up and two lines of tears streaked her face. "I was so frightened. Joseph was making fun of them, but when little Bridget died I finally realized. She hasn't been sick a day in her life. It had to be the bread."

Margaret glanced quickly at the loaf sitting so innocently on her dinner table, then looked back at Bertie. "Careless of me. I should have realized. I'm sorry, Bertie." She placed an arm around her friend and held her for a minute. "Sorry about Bridget and the others. They saved my life."

Bertie looked up and her face had a puzzled expression on it. "It was Cecile that made the bread, but I never expected she was the one."

Margaret tried to remember. "Cecile made it, but all evening it was sitting by the wall. Anyone could have gotten to it. It's not necessarily Cecile's doing."

"Poisoned, after it was baked?"

"That's right. In fact Cecile told me she'd be bringing it two days ago, in front of everyone, so there was plenty of time for the murderer to prepare. They all knew it was there.

Be easy for someone to get the poison into the bread if they planned beforehand. Just a minute.'' She rummaged in her garbage until she found the aluminum-foil wrapper. She smoothed it out and held it to the light. ''See, come here.'' Bertie reluctantly took a step closer. ''All those little pin-pricks of light, that's how the poison got through. It was injected with a syringe.''

''Aluminum foil's always making holes,'' Bertie said, shaking her head. ''Cecile's still the one.'' Bertie took out a handkerchief from her sleeve and dried her eyes. ''Didn't she suggest the bread from the beginning?''

''Yes, but—''

''Don't care what you say. Someone who gives you a loaf of bread full of poison's gotta be guilty.'' She blew her nose loudly. ''No two ways about it. You got any Scotch?''

Margaret almost didn't hear the last words.

''Scotch,'' Bertie repeated. ''I need a drink after what I've been through. Didn't even have time to care for the birds. Just rushed right over. Left them with Joseph.''

Margaret got a bottle out and poured. ''Did you call?''

Bertie took a big swallow and made a funny face. ''Nope. I didn't have a dime. Quicker coming over than trying to make change. Besides''—she finished the drink with another gulp—''take me twenty minutes to find a phone on Broadway that's not been all ripped apart.'' She held the glass out. ''Just a little more, Margaret. It'll calm my nerves.''

Margaret leveled some more Scotch in the glass and sat back.

''Coulda been me too you know,'' Bertie continued. ''I was gonna have some tonight with my liver.'' She started working on her second glass.

''I thought that call was peculiar. Sid gets playful now and then but he always says something. You know what I think—''

Suddenly the phone rang again and both women jumped. Margaret uncapped the bottle and poured some Scotch into her unused teacup. She swallowed it quickly.

"Don't answer it."

"The murderer?" Bertie's eyes were like Ping-Pong balls. Margaret nodded and lit a cigarette. The phone continued to ring as the two women sitting across the table from each other held hands. Finally it stopped.

"There," Margaret said and smiled nervously. "I'm dead."

"Humph," Bertie snorted and finished her drink. "I don't like it. And you thought you were one step ahead. 'Bout to step off a cliff, you were." She pushed back from the table and was about to get up when she thought better of it. "Margaret, I'm not leavin' you. Something might happen."

"Not anymore. I'm supposed to be dead."

"Might come by to check. No, I'm not going." She looked around the apartment quickly. "I'll sleep right on that couch. Just need a blanket."

"But, Bertie—"

"Won't take no for an answer." She yawned. "Wouldn't forgive myself if something happened. No use arguing, just go an' fetch me the cover."

"What about your birds? Joseph won't do anything."

Bertie sighed. "No, don't suppose he will. But they're gone anyway. Now come on, before I change my mind."

Margaret shrugged and got the extra blanket. Then together they cleared the table.

"What about the bread?" Bertie asked. "Want it for evidence?"

"I suppose so," Margaret said, and put it in one of her cupboards. "But not a word of this to the police tomorrow." She looked straight at her friend. "No matter what. If Morley gets wind of it he'll stop everything. I just need one more day until it's over. Chances are this bread was supposed to settle everything. If Morley rushes in and digs up the stones he'll spoil the whole plan. Now promise, not a word.''

Bertie yawned again. ''I promise.'' She sat down on the couch and took off her shoes. ''Don't know why I'm so tired.'' She put her head back and closed her eyes. When Margaret looked around again, she was sleeping. Margaret gently moved her into a reclining position and covered her with the blanket, then turned the lights down, locked the door, and went into her own bedroom.

Poor Bertie, she thought. Never could hold her liquor. I just hope she doesn't make any more noise. She crawled into her own bed. Dead people are not supposed to snore so loudly.

34

By nine o'clock Margaret was sitting comfortably in Morley's office, sipping a coffee and doing the day's crossword puzzle. For the past fifteen minutes she had steadily postponed Morley's questions. "Wait until David gets here," she kept saying. Finally the lieutenant gave up and leaned back with the newspaper.

"Okay, we'll wait," he said and turned to the sports page. "Can you believe it," he said half to himself a minute later. "Bases loaded, bottom of the ninth, and Brown strikes out." He closed the paper in disgust. Margaret looked up from her puzzle.

"Bobby Brown?" She thought for a minute. "Was he batting lefty? He has trouble with that stance." She smiled pleasantly, remembering the grounds keeper's analysis. Morley just looked at her. "They should bat him righty. Goes well to the opposite field that way, don't you think?"

Morley was about to say something when the door opened. Schaeffer looked from one to the other, then went and sat in the chair next to Margaret. His hair was uncombed, his eyes were red, and an unlit cigarette dangled from a corner of his mouth.

"Nothing," he said, "not even a nibble."

Morley slammed the paper down. "Would one of you two mind telling me what the hell's going on? Margaret walks in here, demands I help her, then clams up. Then you walk in looking like yesterday's unrefrigerated leftovers and come out with a half-ass line straight out of a pulp detective novel." He looked from one to the other. "You two guys rehearse this scene?"

"Now, Samuel," Margaret began, "calm yourself. That's no way to talk to someone who's been up all night trying to catch a murderer."

"Well, damn it, fill me in," Morley said, his voice a notch louder than normal. "I run this place. I'd like to know what the hell's going on."

Margaret took a breath. "Well, if you'll just listen for a minute, that's why I'm here. David was watching the garden last night. We thought the murderer would finally move."

"Why?" Morley looked exasperated.

Margaret took her time to explain about the memorial tree and how it was going right over the diamonds and how there was no way the murderer could let that happen. When she was finished, Morley sat silently for a moment, shaking his head slowly from side to side.

"Christ!" he finally said. "You must think that guy's a real jerk. Anyone in his right mind's gotta see it's a perfect setup. The tree right over the diamonds." Morley made a face. "Come on, come on! If I had buried those stones, you know what I'd do? I'd have a go at Margaret, that's all. Then there wouldn't be any more problems, no more little birch trees or whatever. I'm surprised he hasn't tried yet."

Margaret shifted uncomfortably in her seat.

"But he hasn't," Schaeffer said wearily, "and tonight he's gotta bite. It's his last chance."

"Yeah, yeah." Morley lit a cigarette and blew a cloud up to the fluorescent light. "I don't like it, that's all. This kid's no dummy. He was cool when it came to staying with the closing of the garden. He didn't move then, what if he won't budge now?"

"I give you my word, Samuel," Margaret said, "that if nothing happens tonight, tomorrow you can have your diamonds back."

"Thanks." Morley grinned. "Very generous of you. That also means you'll have to take a vacation for a while."

Margaret looked down at the floor. "I understand."

Morley swiveled toward Schaeffer. "You willing to give it another night?"

Schaeffer nodded. "I'll get a few hours sleep this afternoon. But I need Jacobson and the equipment tonight. It's too much for one person alone, especially in my condition."

"What about today?" Morley asked. "You can't let her walk around and be a target."

Both men turned toward Margaret. There was a moment of silence.

"I do have one little errand to do," she said. "I want to check on something in the garden. But then I can stay home all afternoon if you want."

"We can put Staunton on her," Schaeffer said, "just to be sure."

"But not tonight," Margaret said quickly. "I want to be there. Since you'll be two, I won't be in the way. Last night was different."

Schaeffer rolled his eyes.

"Under no circumstances." Morley shook his head. "You're crazy! We're taking a chance with you this afternoon. No way we're going to do it tonight. Sorry,

Margaret." He turned to Schaeffer. "Tell Staunton to follow her home then stay on duty outside the door."

"You're locking me in?" Margaret was shocked.

"Something like that."

"But . . ."

"Unh-unh. You want this, you gotta play by the rules, my rules. Now," Morley said, "you've narrowed it down?" He took a pencil out of his top drawer and found a clean scrap of paper. "Who are they?"

She smiled faintly, looked first at Schaeffer, then at Morley, and carefully refolded her crossword.

"My rules," she said. "You'll find out tomorrow."

"Now wait . . ."

"Nope." She stood up. "I can be just as stubborn. You men sometimes are worse than children—locking me in. Ought to be ashamed . . ."

"It's for your own good. Now, who is it?" Morley faced her. She shook her head.

"Sorry. Either we trust each other or we don't. You've made your choice. You'll have to wait." She moved to the door. Morley followed her.

"I've played some crazy games in my time," he said, "but this ranks right up there. Don't forget, this is your last night." He looked at Margaret for a second, then opened the door brusquely.

"One day," Margaret said to Schaeffer outside, "he'll lay off that gruff exterior and show everyone how nice a man he can be."

"Yeah," Schaeffer said. "Don't hold your breath."

Margaret put her hand on Schaeffer's arm. "Seriously, David, can't you take me with you this evening? He'll never know. After all that I've done, to be left out of it. Something's bound to happen."

"I'm sorry," the young policeman said. "Morley's the word around here. I can't, especially with Staunton assigned.

He'd never go for it. Sam'd hear about it a minute after you walked out the door.''

"There's nothing you can do? I'm going to read about it in the morning papers like everyone else?''

Schaeffer looked at her closely for a moment. Finally he made up his mind. "Wait here. You can't be with us, but there may be something. I'll be right back.'' He turned and walked down the precinct's narrow corridor. She saw him enter one of the rooms at the back. It took a good ten minutes, but he finally returned carrying two small cases. He motioned her outside.

"What is it?'' she asked.

"Walkie-talkie. Most powerful we got and tuned to each other. Property clerk wanted to know why I needed them.''

"What'd you tell him?''

"Told him it was none of his business.'' Schaeffer smiled. "It helps to have drinking buddies around the office. Come on, I'll show you how it works.''

They started walking slowly down the block as Schaeffer took one of the radios out of the case.

"This button here turns it on. Now to talk, just press this and speak into that round mike. Let up on the button to listen. It's very simple. Here.'' He handed her the radio.

"I don't know, David.'' She looked at it suspiciously. "I never used one of these before.'' She touched one of the black knobs. "What's this do?''

"That changes the frequency. Leave that where it is.''

"Can't you just take me?''

"This is the best I can do. I'll call you every half hour and tell you how many crooks we've caught.''

"Very funny. Can I try it?''

"Go ahead. I'll walk down the block.'' Margaret turned on the power and immediately the air around her was filled with static.

Now what? she thought.

"Can you hear me?" Schaeffer's voice barked out of the speaker.

"Oh, my, yes. I mean"—she pushed down on her talk button—"yes, David, I can hear you. You're a bit loud. You'll wake up all my neighbors." She waited for his response but nothing came. After a minute she looked up the block and saw he was motioning with his thumb. "Oh, I forgot." She took her thumb off and Schaeffer came through clearly.

"The button to the right of the mike is the volume." She turned it down and called back.

"How about you, David? Can you hear me now?"

"Loud and clear. Think you got it?"

She smiled to herself and switched her thumb to the talk button. "Roger. A-OK. Over and out." She switched off the power and started walking toward him. When she arrived, he had a funny expression on his face.

"What was that?"

"Oh, something I heard once in an old John Wayne World War II movie. It wasn't appropriate?"

"Very." He grinned. "These things are supposed to work over a couple of miles, so it should carry. We should start the surveillance around seven o'clock tonight. I won't call you until it gets dark. Here." He unfolded a creased brown paper bag from his pocket. "Carry it in that. It's less obvious. Now." He took her arm and steered her back in the direction of the precinct. "If you'll wait a minute, I'll get Staunton. Just promise me one thing."

"What's that?"

"Plan on spending a quiet night at home. It'll be healthier."

"Seems like I don't have much of a choice. Is there anything on at least?"

"Yeah. *Kind Hearts and Coronets.*"

"Damn," she said. "Seen it twice."

35

On her way to the garden Margaret stopped off at her favorite candy store and purchased one of the smaller crossword-puzzle books. It was going to be a long afternoon cooped up in her apartment. Might as well have something to do, she thought. As she left, she noticed Staunton a half block behind her, dressed in street clothes and trying to look inconspicuous. Nowhere near as good an actor as David, she mused. He didn't have that casual, seedy style. He looked more like an insurance broker on a lunch break.

The garden gate was locked when she arrived, but after a minute she opened it and eased herself inside. She looked around carefully. The tree was still positioned by the wall. Already a small sparrow had found a comfortable resting place on one of the branches. Aside from an occasional sound from the young bird, everything was quiet. She walked slowly to the rear and opened the tool locker. She remembered where the bottle was, in the back on the left. Her hand found it immediately and she knew the answer before she looked. She could tell by its weight that the container of Malathion was nearly empty. She opened the cap and saw there was no more than a quarter of an inch of fluid left in the bottom. Almost a half pint had been pumped into the corn bread.

"Just as I thought," she murmured. Slowly she reached up and placed the bottle prominently on the top of the locker, fully visible from the street. There, she thought, that'll take away any uncertainty about my present state of health. Now there's only one alternative. She closed the locker door lightly, dusted her hands off, and turned to go.

"Whatcha doin'?"

Margaret jumped, nearly dropping the crossword book and brown paper bag with the radio Schaeffer had given her.

"Oh, John." She caught her breath. "You scared me."

The young boy looked suspiciously at Margaret. "Didn't think we were supposed to meet till tomorrow," he said.

"We're not," Margaret recovered. "I was just checking something." She glanced quickly past the tall boy's shoulder and saw Staunton at the edge of the chicken-wire fence. His hand was inside his jacket pocket. She looked back at John Kee. "What are you doing here?"

"Just passing by. Sometimes I detour to make sure everything's okay. After what happened with the flowers . . ."

"Mmm yes," Margaret said and moved quickly past him. "Always pays to be careful. I must remember that. You coming?"

The youth followed her out of the garden and watched as Margaret relocked the gate. Staunton casually sauntered a few steps away.

"I got all the stuff for the tree," Kee said. "I'll bring it to-morrow."

"Good." Margaret smiled. "Nothing more to do till then." She started to walk away. "See you."

She left John with a puzzled expression on his face. He looked back once at the locker then finally headed off in the opposite direction toward Broadway.

36

STAUNTON followed Margaret into her building.

"Everything okay?" he asked roughly.

She glowered. "Of course everything is all right. You really don't have to hang around."

"Sorry, Mrs. Binton. Orders. I'll be outside your door. I won't be in the way."

"All day?" Margaret glanced at her watch. "Well, as long as you're staying, come in and have something to eat. Maybe tonight I'll make a chicken."

He shook his head. "Thanks, I'm on a diet. If you don't mind, I'll just sit in your living room."

Margaret sighed, pushed her floor number, and the two of them rode up in the elevator together. They entered her apartment and Margaret closed the door.

"Well, I'll make the chicken anyway," she said. "Once you smell it . . ." Her voice trailed off as she headed for the kitchen. Staunton heard the clatter of pots and pans. He went immediately to the windows and checked to see that they were locked. Then he double-bolted the door and took an appraising glance around. Only then did he walk to the easy chair and sit down.

Margaret poked her head out of the kitchen. "You don't mind if I call my friend Bertie and invite her over for dinner? That chicken's too big for the two of us."

"Go right ahead," Staunton said and opened up a newspaper. "Just pretend I'm not here."

"In that case," Margaret said bluntly, "you'll have to move. You're sitting in my favorite chair."

Schaeffer watched from one of the stoops at the end of the block as Jacobson pulled the TV repair van into the spot next to the garden. It was 7:15. The fence was locked and except for an occasional gust of wind that set the corn swaying, nothing inside was moving. Schaeffer walked slowly down the block and stopped casually by the side of the van. He looked around once, then opened the door and hopped inside. Jacobson was just beginning on a tuna fish salad sandwich.

"Christ, already with the food," Schaeffer said.

"I figure it's gonna be a long one. There're more in the back."

Schaeffer unstrapped the walkie-talkie from the panel in front of him and moved with it into the rear of the truck. He sat down opposite the one-way glass and leaned back.

"I'll take the first hour," he called out. "Nothing's gonna happen for a while but you never know. I promised Margaret I'd start calling her at nine." He looked out the window at the garden and the birch tree resting against the side wall. After a few seconds he focused on the cleared flat spot above the diamonds. "Then again," he sighed, "he might not come at all. Where're those sandwiches?"

"Underneath the tear gas cannisters," Jacobson said and bit down on his sandwich. "You got a choice, chicken salad or tuna."

*   *   *

"You sure I can't give you some chicken?" Margaret said, turning to Staunton on the couch.

He shook his head now for the third time. "The cup of coffee was all I need." He raised the *Time* magazine again and Margaret turned back to Bertie.

"Never understand young men and diets," she said. "Oscar was never on a diet a day in his life. Ate like a horse and stayed the same one hundred eighty-four."

"And now they're jogging everywhere," Bertie added. "Get their little shorts on, go around the block a few times. Disgraceful the way they frighten you. One near crashed me flat last week." Bertie pried at a chicken wing for a few moments, shaking her head. "Indecent too, all those knobby knees." Staunton shifted on the couch and laughed behind his magazine. Margaret poured some coffee.

"Psst. I still think it's Cecile," Bertie said, leaning forward.

Margaret held a finger to her lips. "We won't know until tomorrow for sure. You're forgetting that each one had the opportunity with the cake."

"But you said yourself she's the only one that didn't know Luiz from before. Came to the garden by accident! Humph. Offers to help one day out of the blue." Bertie raised an eyebrow. "That's not suspicious? And those groups she belongs to . . ."

"True." Margaret took a sip of coffee. "But what about Jerry's brother in the diamond business, and the argument he had with Luiz, or for that matter John's leaving the gate open and the Phillips screwdriver. As far as motive is concerned, his is clear-cut. I told you about his uncle in Korea. Then there's Vinnie and his gang of friends, all of whom have been in trouble before, or Peter, who for some reason comes to work in the garden even though he hates getting dirty. Don't you find that strange? None of them is above suspicion, Bertie, and you shouldn't jump to conclusions."

"I'm not jumping," Bertie said. "It's the way I feel, that's all." She looked crestfallen.

Margaret looked at her watch. "Well, it's time." She reached over, opened a drawer, and switched on the walkie-talkie. A low level of static came out. "But there's no telling how long it will take. That's why I said before you ought to go home after a while. I'll call you first thing in the morning."

Bertie looked tentatively at the radio. "I'll stay for a little bit anyway. Beats watching TV." She looked back at Margaret and frowned. "But what a backache I had this morning. Been a while since I slept on couches. What's that thing? Some kind of a radio?"

Margaret nodded and nearly spilled the coffee as it crackled into life and Schaeffer's voice came through loud and clear. Both women leaned closer to the machine.

"Margaret, it's nine o'clock. Can you hear me?"

Margaret reached and pressed the button. "Yes, David, I'm here. Where are you?"

"In front of the garden. So far nothing, but it's still early. Where's Staunton?"

"On the couch, reading a magazine." She smiled. "I tried to give him something to eat but he says he's on a diet."

"Try junk food," Schaeffer said. "He's a sucker for Hostess Twinkies. How about you? All okay?"

"Yes. Bertie's here too but she'll be leaving shortly."

"Fine. I'll call back at nine thirty unless something happens first. I don't want the extra noise so I'm turning my machine off."

"Okay, bye . . ." Margaret winked at Bertie, who had been listening to the exchange with great interest. "I mean . . . Roger, over and out." She released the talk button. "Just a little something David and I cooked up."

"You're always full of surprises," Bertie said, and leaned back. "Don't mind if I do have some more coffee."

*   *   *

Schaeffer called every half hour for the next four hours with the same story. Nothing moving in the garden and little traffic in the street. The novelty of the calls had worn off after the first few hours for Bertie, who had long since begun to yawn. It was already two hours past her normal bedtime. The television was on and Staunton was just barely keeping awake on the couch.

After Schaeffer's one o'clock call, Bertie got up slowly and reached for her sweater.

"Could go on all night like this," she said. "I'd best go. Back's in bad enough shape as it is." Staunton shifted on the couch and looked at her with one eye. Margaret got up, turned down the television, and walked Bertie to the door.

"I'm feeling sleepy myself," Margaret admitted. "But don't worry. I'll let you know in the morning. Be careful walking home."

"It's only a few blocks." Bertie kissed her friend good-bye.

When Margaret turned back into the room, Staunton had his eyes shut. She looked at the clock in the kitchen and sighed. One fifteen. She was beginning to feel anxious. No, it's still early, she assured herself. Plenty of time. A whole night. And she walked back and adjusted the volume on the TV set. Staunton didn't move. Let him sleep, she thought. Poor boy looked tired when he came in. She pulled the easy chair closer to the set, put the walkie-talkie on her lap, and sank back down. She answered Schaeffer's 1:30 call promptly, was a little slow on the two o'clock one, and barely heard the 2:30 buzz. When she did, Schaeffer sounded exasperated.

"What's wrong, Margaret? Took five minutes to get you."

"Sorry, David. I guess I must have dozed a little."

"You want me to stop calling?"

"No, I'll try to stay awake. I'll let you know." She

yawned and noticed the television set was now flickering. "Still nothing?"

"Like a morgue."

"David, I don't know what to say . . . ."

"Save it," he said. "Call you later."

"Thank you, David. Next one's three?"

"Right."

"Okay, bye." She put the machine back in her lap and thought for a long time about the slowly flickering TV. It was too much of an effort to get up and stop it. Besides, the lights were pretty, the motion so rhythmic, it reminded her briefly of waves at the ocean: Coney Island, Rockaway, Atlantic City, Cape Cod, Rye. In five minutes she was sound asleep.

There was movement on the fire escape. A figure shifted from a sitting to a kneeling position and slowly thrust two hands between the heavy iron bars protecting Margaret's kitchen window. The locked window refused to budge. The figure reached into a pocket and withdrew a glass cutter. In the bottom corner of the lower window a two-inch-square cut was made, and after a little tap, the glass popped out, tinkling lightly in the kitchen sink. Staunton moved uneasily but his eyes stayed closed.

From a plastic bag four two-foot sections of curtain rod were withdrawn and screwed tightly together. Along one side of this eight-foot rod was now taped plastic tubing with the far end curving slightly downward. One end the figure mouthed while the rod was inserted through the square hole in the window. This obscene mechanical anteater probed not for food, but on top of the stove toward the pilot-light hole. After several missed attempts the plastic tube slipped through the tiny hole. The figure held the position for a second, took a deep breath, and blew. The pilot could not be seen, so there was only one way to tell if the operation was success-

ful. The rod was now balanced on one of the burner knobs, and pushed. The knob turned ninety degrees and the intruder waited for the accompanying rush of flame. Nothing happened—just the faintest hiss of escaping gas could be heard through the small opening in the glass. It took another three minutes of manipulating the rod to turn on all the other burners and stove. The hiss turned into a shushing sound.

Schaeffer got wearily out of the driver's seat and lumbered into the back. He tapped Jacobson on the shoulder and motioned him to move.

"My turn. It's three o'clock."

Jacobson smiled thinly and just shook his head.

"Ain't this a bitch," he said. "I can tell you twenty things I'd rather be doing than sitting in this lousy van, and eighteen of them involve a bed."

"You're getting paid. Who else do you know gets paid for sitting on his ass all night? Come on."

Jacobson shifted over. "You think she's right?"

Schaeffer shrugged and settled down in front of the window. "Who knows? I can't think this time of night." He scratched his beard and looked down into his coffee cup. "We outta coffee?"

"Yeah, I had that last cup around two thirty, watching that hooker. You'd think she'd find a better spot for business."

"Who, Labelle?" Schaeffer chuckled. "She's been working the side streets since I came on five years ago. Always connects." He took a deep puff and looked skeptically at the radio by his side. "Think I should call her again?"

"Margaret?"

"Yeah." He fingered the on switch. "Last time I think I woke her up."

"Nah. Do her a favor and let her sleep. Nothing's happening anyway."

Schaeffer removed his hand from the radio and looked out

the window. The garden looked as peaceful as a Currier and
Ives print. "Maybe Morley was right. He figured the murderer wouldn't bite."

"He's such a goddamn skeptic." Jacobson shifted lower
into one of the front seats and rubbed his eyes. "Holler if
you need me."

"Yeah, sure." Schaeffer turned and watched as the moon-
light played off the different plants in the garden, changing
the shapes with the slightest movements. Morley sure was a
skeptic, he thought, but not often wrong. He considered the
glowing end of his butt for a moment, then crushed it out on
the floor and put it in his empty cup. What the hell. He
reached out, flicked on the switch, and put the radio to his
mouth.

Margaret felt something in her lap, more the vibration of
the speaker than the actual sound it made. It was something
distant, down a corridor, way out of reach. The corridor itself
was spinning, impossible to get through. She struggled and in
her mind stumbled and fell to the end. Everything turned
green. Junglelike tomato plants enveloped her. Tendrils of
dense creepers reached out and caught in her hair, pulling her
down, spinning her again. Everywhere was the smell of
dense marsh gas. She gasped. Between two gigantic trees she
saw a hand holding a sparkling glass syringe reach out and
stab violently at a foil-covered object, again and again. She
tried to look away, refocus, forget. But there was something
demanding her attention, calling her back.

She had the feeling she was being singled out. Not just
anyone, it was specifically for . . . "Margaret!" She tried to
concentrate, to stop the spinning, to make all the hazy illu-
sions coalesce into something she understood. But she
couldn't find a foothold. Everything kept changing, shifting,
receding. There was a key to it all, something she could do,

some simple trick. What? Someone calling now . . . Who? Oscar? Find out. Names familiar . . . need the key. Still dizzy, she barely lifted open one eye and saw the radio on her lap.

"Margaret, are you awake?"

"Margaret," she whispered her name curiously.

"This is the last time. If you're awake, answer me."

Answer, she thought. What's it mean? She struggled to get the other eye open and lay exhausted against the back of the chair. The radio was silent. Button, she dimly remembered. Push the button. Her hand edged forward and found the machine. The edges of her newfound vision were blackening, like an ink stain merging toward a center. So many, so many things to push. Which one? She tried one. It was an impossible effort to get it down. She used all her strength, gasping from the strain. Did it move? Was it the right one? What was that smell? She had only a second left before passing out. The black stain was now an abyss in front of her with only the tiniest pinprick of light. She pushed her mouth together and barely whispered a single word.

Schaeffer's hand was on the off button when he heard the change in static pitch and then the tiniest of sounds. He wasn't even sure he had heard correctly. He spoke again into the machine for another ten seconds, calling her name, but still there was nothing. Was he only imagining it, listening to his own anxieties? Had he really heard her call for help?

"Margaret, damn it, come in!" His voice was loud enough to raise Jacobson.

"What . . ."

Schaeffer didn't wait. He jumped into the driver's seat and started the engine.

"Hey. . . !"

"Something's happened." He shifted into gear and without even looking, roared out of the spot. "Hang on." He made the turn onto Broadway on two wheels and got up to thirty-five miles an hour within a block and a half.

"This thing got a siren?"

Jacobson fiddled for a minute under the dash. "Shit, it's here somewhere." Finally he pulled a lever and from under the hood came the shrill sound of a klaxon. Even at that time of night Broadway had a few cars and Schaeffer narrowly missed two on Eighty-eighth Street. He finally clipped a third on Eighty-seventh but didn't stop. They screeched to a halt for an agonizing fifteen seconds behind a bus trying to pull over, then Schaeffer goosed it back up to thirty-five for the last few blocks. He was almost out of the truck before it stopped. Jacobson was right at his side.

"Open up, goddamnit." Schaeffer pounded on the front door until he woke up the night elevator operator. The old man advanced slowly, his hair all disheveled and his shirt rumpled from being slept in. His eyes were still trying to focus.

"Police," Schaeffer yelled. "Open the door."

The elevator man took one look at the bearded man waving the gun and took a step backward in fear. The door remained locked. Jacobson reached into his back pocket and withdrew his I.D. card, but the man stayed rooted to the spot four feet away, paralyzed.

"The hell with it," Schaeffer cursed, put the muzzle of his .38 against the glass, and pulled the trigger. The shot shattered the front pane and he reached in and undid the latch himself. He didn't notice the long thin cut he got withdrawing his hand, or the spattering of blood that followed him as he ran to the elevator.

"What floor?" Jacobson yelled.

"Christ, I can't remember." He wheeled around and advanced on the old man.

"Margaret Binton. What floor . . . quick!''

The old man swallowed hard and shook his head. Schaeffer lifted the pistol and pointed it between his eyes.

"What floor, Pop? You've got two seconds.''

The elevator man closed his eyes. "Five.''

"Thanks.'' He ran to the elevator and Jacobson slammed the door behind him. His landing on the fifth floor was way off but he opened the door anyway. Schaeffer jumped the two feet and scooted to the left. He remembered Margaret's apartment.

Even before he got there, he could smell the gas in the hall. He tried the handle once, then stepped back and raised the gun. Jacobson's hand clamped over his.

"No! You might spark it.''

"Right.'' The two of them threw their bodies against the door until the latch started to loosen. It was another minute before the catch gave way and the door swung in. Schaeffer's eyes started tearing three feet inside, but he still managed to see Staunton sprawled on the couch. His color was not good. He motioned to Jacobson, then went looking for Margaret. He found her on the floor in front of the television set, the walkie-talkie at her feet still emitting a steady noise. He grabbed her by the arms and dragged her outside and down the hall. Jacobson was right behind him with Staunton.

"We too late?''

"I don't know. Cut the gas . . . give me some air.'' Jacobson ran back into the apartment with a handkerchief in front of his face, turned off the stove, and quickly opened the windows. As he did so, he noticed the little cutout square in the kitchen. When he came back, he saw Schaeffer working over Margaret on the floor. He dropped to his knees, pulled back Staunton's head, and started giving mouth-to-mouth resuscitation. The only noise in the hallway was the syncopated breathing of the two policemen as they worked over the two victims. Staunton's color came back slowly and he opened his eyes. He looked around him curiously, then up at the familiar face.

"Jake, what are you doing here?"

"Christ, thank God. That's one," Jacobson said. "I'll call an ambulance. Stay there," he told Staunton. "Don't move."

When he came back the second time from Margaret's apartment, Schaeffer was still working over her. A thick layer of perspiration covered his body and his face was a scarlet from the exertion. It was almost three minutes since he had brought her out and still no movement.

"They'll be right here," Jacobson said. "Got a special priority." He bent down and felt for Margaret's pulse. He frowned, kept searching, then looked into her eyes. "Keep going, I think I feel something."

Schaeffer was methodical. Thirty breaths a minute. The blood seeping from his hand made a small puddle next to her shoulder, but he didn't notice. Her face was all he looked at and it was still a pasty yellow. Slowly, very slowly, it began to take on some color. At the five-minute mark Jacobson yelled, "You got her." But Schaeffer kept working, right up until Margaret's breathing returned at a steady rate and she lost the chalkiness from her cheeks. Then he rolled over and leaned against the wall, exhausted. It took a moment, but he finally caught his breath.

"Christ!"

"Hey, you're bleeding."

Schaeffer looked down. "Musta scratched it on the door. Hospital will fix it up when I get there. You'd better go back. I'll take this end."

"You sure?"

"I'm all right." He propped himself up. "No one's on the garden, damn it. Go ahead, get moving. Call me later."

Jacobson gave Margaret a last quick look and saw she was

just beginning to stir. Then he rushed back into the elevator and brought it down. He passed the ambulance attendants in the lobby as they were entering. He pointed upstairs.

"Fifth floor and hurry it."

"Any dead?"

"No, man, but you couldn't get much closer."

The hospital room they put Margaret in had three beds, but hers was the only one occupied. Staunton refused to be admitted but was sitting instead in one of the chairs in Margaret's room, watching her. Schaeffer, with his hand bandaged, finally walked in from the emergency room. He took a look at Margaret.

"She'll be all right?" he asked softly.

"They want her to rest for a day. She can leave tomorrow," Staunton said.

"Don't worry about it," Schaeffer whispered. "As long as nothing happened."

"Yeah, but . . ."

"I said forget it." He lit a cigarette awkwardly with his bandaged hand and paced back and forth.

"Jacobson called."

"He did? When?" Schaeffer wheeled around and looked at the clock over the bed. It read 3:55.

"A few minutes after you went downstairs to get your hand fixed. Maybe ten minutes ago."

"What'd he say?"

"Said he'd be right over. That you shouldn't leave yet."

"Goddamnit!" Schaeffer made a fist. "We blew it! I knew . . ."

"What?"

Just then Jacobson walked in. His hands and nails were covered with dirt. Schaeffer took one look and sat down heavily.

"Empty?"

Jacobson nodded. "A hole about three feet deep. Dirt sprayed everywhere. Musta been in a real hurry."

"What's he talking about?" Staunton asked.

"The diamonds!" Schaeffer said in exasperation. "The diamonds are gone."

37

MARGARET opened her eyes later that afternoon and tried to orient herself. She was in a strange bed, curtained partitions separated her from the window, and a faint smell of disinfectant was in the air. She shifted her head and saw Morley looking down at her. She smiled faintly.

"I'm not going to say 'where am I' because I think I know."

"And damn lucky too," Morley said. "You almost didn't make it."

"Gas?"

He nodded. "All done through a little hole in the window."

She groaned and raised herself to a sitting position. "My head feels like an old rotted tree trunk. How's Officer Staunton?"

"I gave him the day off," Morley growled. "I should have given him a year instead."

"It's not his fault." Margaret tried to smile. "He did make sure the windows were locked. I guess the stuffiness made him drowsy." She reached over to the night table where she saw a pack of cigarettes.

"David leave these?"

"Yeah, he figured you'd want them when you woke up." Morley lit one for her and watched as she inhaled deeply. He waited a minute before continuing. "You know the diamonds are gone."

She knitted her forehead. "That will be a problem. No telling where they'll be now."

"Tell us who it is, Margaret. With any luck we'll toss his place and find the stones. As it is now this is going to be one hell of an embarrassing mess if it ever gets out."

Margaret shook her head slowly. "If I tell you who I think it is, and I certainly don't have any proof, chances are you'll never find the stones again. A lot of trouble was taken to conceal them up till now and I don't think you'll find them lying around an apartment. Besides"—she winked—"I have an extra trick up my sleeve."

"What can you do now? The stones are gone." Morley gestured impatiently. "Be reasonable."

"I'm being perfectly reasonable. What happened last night was unfortunate, but it doesn't change everything. The murderer very cleverly avoided the trap we set, but not entirely. In a few days I'll have the proof I need."

"How? He left nothing, no footprints, pieces of clothing, fingerprints."

"I know. A very careful criminal. But mark my words, Lieutenant, not careful enough to avoid making a serious mistake."

"What?"

"You'll see. Meanwhile, what time is it?" She struggled up higher in bed. "The tree is going in at six."

"Oh, no, you're not leaving the hospital."

"Certainly. Everything has to look normal for the time

being. I'll just take a few of those aspirins to clear my head. Now where did that nurse put my dress?''

Morley moved forward and put a hand out. ''Margaret, you're not leaving.''

''Who said so?''

''Me, and a couple of strong policemen standing outside your door. Now come on and get back into bed. These floors are cold without slippers on.''

''Lieutenant, you're impossible.'' She sat reluctantly back on the bed and shifted the covers over her legs. ''You're always cooping me up.''

''For your own good. Last night you were almost killed. You want more?'' He turned to go. ''I'll drop by tomorrow morning, see how you're getting along.''

''What a bore.'' She sat back and stared straight ahead. ''Can't even see my friends that I see every day. After all, it's just a little headache.''

''Ask them to visit,'' Morley said.

''Through that honor guard?''

''I'll tell them.'' He opened the door.

''How long do you figure you'll keep me here?'' She sounded hurt.

Morley smiled. ''Until you're better . . . and tell me who killed Luiz and took the diamonds. In the meantime I've got to figure out what to do with this mess.''

''Humph,'' she snorted. ''In that case I'd better get Bertie over here.''

''. . . And don't forget the lamp,'' Margaret repeated. ''That's important.''

''But I thought the hospital had enough lights,'' Bertie objected.

''Never mind, we'll need it. And hurry.'' She replaced the phone on its hook and lay back on the soft pillows. A little grin touched the corners of her mouth. "Coop me up, will he? We'll see about that."

She didn't have long to wait. Less than an hour later Bertie came marching past the guards at the door, carrying a little bouquet of flowers and a small table lamp. She was wearing her summer straw hat with the gauze and feathers and a rust-colored double-knit suit. Margaret could not have been more pleased to see anyone.

"Quick, Bertie," she said, jumping up, "get undressed and get into bed!"

"What?"

"One old lady is just like another to some of these nurses. They won't notice the switch for hours. I just hope I can fool Morley's watchdogs." She looked askance at Bertie's figure. "Size twelve is it?"

"But . . ."

"Never mind. It'll have to do. I can guarantee it's a soft bed and all the bouillon you can drink for free." She started helping Bertie off with her jacket.

"Margaret, wait a minute. What's going on? I thought you were sick."

"Of course not. Simply a minor headache. But they won't let me leave and I've got an appointment."

"But . . ."

"No 'buts,' Bertie. It's taking up time. Lord, I don't think I'll ever fit into those shoes. Maybe I can get away with using mine." She looked in the closet and made a face. "I knew it, Morley had them lifted. Well, I can't go barefoot. Come on, dear, off with them. That's right. Now the skirt."

In another ten minutes the switch was complete. Margaret was dressed in Bertie's clothes, including the hat, and her friend was resting comfortably in the bed. An empty ice bag covered her forehead and most of her eyes.

"See if you can stick it out until tomorrow," Margaret

said. "I'd better stay with a friend tonight just in case Morley comes back."

"I don't like this at all," Bertie said. "Where are you going?"

"Don't worry, dear." Margaret bent over to adjust the straps on the black shoes. "I'm just going to plant a tree. Then it's a matter of waiting. Probably a day, no more. Now where's that lamp?"

"You want that too?"

"Of course. If they have any doubts about it being the same person coming out, they'll look at that and not bother with the rest. It's the little accessories that mark the individual these days, not always the face. Now be a good patient and drink all your soup." She bent over and kissed Bertie on the cheek. "Tomorrow it will all be over and we'll celebrate at Tip Toe Inn."

"Tip Toe went out of business years ago."

"Whatever," Margaret said, and picked up the lamp. "Here goes . . ."

38

THEY were all waiting for her in the garden when she arrived. None of the young gardeners looked shocked as Margaret came through the fence and walked carefully over. In her hands she carried a bouquet of fresh dahlias.

"Someone already dug the hole," Peter said. "No one wants to take the credit though. Lookit, they did a lousy job." Margaret set the flowers down and walked over to where he pointed. There was the gaping hole and strewn all about it the wild plants from the reservoir with their roots exposed, withered and dead in the full day of sunshine. Wordlessly, Margaret went over to the tool cabinet, removed a rake, and very deliberately started collecting the loose dead plants into a pile off to the side. In three minutes there was not a single piece of ground cover around the hole. She stopped and looked up. "Now it's clear. I think we can move the tree. It would have been awful to plant it amidst all that mess. Jerry, perhaps you and Peter could bring it over. John and Cecile, could you drive in the stakes? Vinnie, when they're finished filling the hole, you can wire the tree so it won't blow over. As for the plaque"—she reached into her handbag and drew out the thin bronze plate—"we can do that last. John, you brought the bolts?"

He nodded.

"Good." She glanced up to the sky. "We still have plenty of time."

Everyone set to work. After the tree was put in place, Peter took a sharp knife from his pocket and cut the burlap so that the roots could branch out. Cecile held one of the long stakes while John brought the back of the shovel down against it. It was the only real noise in the garden and it echoed against the walls like repeating shots. Vinnie waited until the dirt was packed down, put his radio on the ground, and began wiring between the stakes and the tree. In twenty minutes the operation was completed. After John secured the plaque, everyone stepped back to admire the sturdy little birch.

"Very nice," Margaret said and bent over to place the dahlias at the base of the tree. When she stood up, a little tear was showing at the corner of her eye.

"Ain'tcha gonna say something?" Peter asked softly.

She nodded, took out a tissue, and blew her nose. After a minute she started in a very controlled voice.

"We plant this tree in Luiz's memory. In some way he helped us all. He gave us a refuge, a place to come and work and be at peace." She looked at each one carefully. "And because of the kind of man he was, he also touched our lives personally. He showed us how to be generous and caring." She took out her tissue again and dabbed at her eye. "Then someone killed him. We will all suffer by that awful crime, and miss his presence. This tree is only one way of remembering. We'll each hold our own special memories long after we stop coming here." She took a step forward and touched the tree lightly. "This is the first memorial tree I've ever planted. I hope it's my last.'' She turned to the side. ''Would anyone else like to say something?''

There was a hesitation, then Vinnie stepped awkwardly forward. As a concession to the solemnity of the occasion, he removed his mirrored glasses. ''All I want to say,'' Vinnie began, ''is it's a cryin' shame. Guy like that gets it when he don't deserve it. I mean, whoever did it oughta be hung.'' He looked around quickly, then stepped back.

''Yeah,'' Peter Muñoz added. He glanced down at his feet for a second. ''He was a prince, man. Guys like that don't come around too often, especially up in the *barrio*. Everyone's out hustling for himself.'' He nodded at the tree. ''He was one that wasn't.''

''A class act,'' Jerry agreed. ''As they say where I come from, a real *mensch*.'' He bent down, picked up a handful of dirt, and tossed it lightly at the base of the tree. ''I never thought about religion much, but losing Luiz was different.'' He forced a smile. ''I said a prayer for him in temple last week.'' He looked around. ''It was the least I could do.''

''You know,'' John Kee interrupted the momentary silence, ''more than anything else he was like a member of the family—somewhere in between a brother and a father. I felt closer to him than I did to most of my relatives. I'll remember . . .'' he said and his voice seemed a little shaky, ''I'll remember him not only as a friend, but as much, much more.''

''Amen,'' Cecile said and took a half step forward. ''There ain't no more can be said . . . 'cept maybe that the man knew more about cooperation and working together than the whole United States government. He had a knack of getting people together,'' she added, ''and it's a shame, 'cause here we are, and he's gone.'' She stepped back. No one spoke. As they watched, another sparrow circled the tree and landed in a top branch.

"If it's any consolation," Margaret said, breaking the stillness, "the police think they know who murdered him."

"What!" Jerry grabbed her arm. "Who is he?" The others crowded around her.

"I don't know very much"—she shrugged—"just that they have a lead, that's all. Something happened last night . . ."

"What?" This time it was John Kee.

"I couldn't say. My friend will let me know. He works at the Eighty-first Precinct." She moved to the side and saw Sid waiting for her right outside the gate. Right on time, she thought. She took one last look behind her. "I suppose it's time to go. We're all finished here."

"So they haven't caught him yet?" Cecile asked. "It's just a theory?"

Margaret moved past them and started for the gate. "Yes, just a theory," she said. "But they're usually very careful. If they didn't have something, they wouldn't have let it out." She reached the gate. "Maybe we'll know something tomorrow." She went through, grabbed Sid's hand, and started walking toward Broadway.

She was over a block away when Vinnie caught up with her. He looked anxious.

"This gotta be fast," he said. "I don't want him to see me."

"Who?"

"Never mind. I seen something last night I thought was strange. What you said about the cops rang a bell. But first I gotta check it out. I don't want to point no fingers at the wrong guy." He looked around again quickly. "And I think I got some evidence. He dropped something. Leastwise, I think it's his. Won't take me long to match it."

Margaret looked at him curiously. "Vinnie, what is it?"

"Not now." He started to move away. "Where can I reach you tonight?"

She tugged at her friend's sleeve. "What's the number, Sid?"

"Five five five–six seven six three," he said, "but what's going . . ."

"You got that, Vinnie?"

"Yeah. I'll call. Soon's I know." Vinnie turned and ran back toward the garden.

"What was all that about?" Sid asked.

"I haven't the faintest idea," Margaret said. "It's nothing I'd planned on."

39

SID lived in one of the older buildings along West End Avenue, a pre–World War I queen bravely fighting off efforts to convert it into a cooperative. His two-bedroom apartment on a high floor was a rent control steal at $115 a month. He'd lived there for twenty-five years, almost one third of his life, the last ten of them alone. And now, even though he rattled around in the big apartment, through huge rooms that only emphasized his isolation, he knew he couldn't afford to leave the place. It was the only bargain he had ever had, and one he was locked into even though he knew he would have been happier in some cosy one-room studio.

But Margaret's presence next to him in the large living room that evening was a pleasure. Together they seemed to fill up the space. She browsed through his old magazines while he poured the drinks. He didn't usually have company, and he began the conversation when he came back by apologizing for the condition of things. There were layers upon layers of mementos lying about.

"Oh, come on!" Margaret made a motion with her hand and put the magazine down. "Looks perfectly fine to me. Maybe needs a little dusting here and there." She took a sip of her sherry. "I know you men can't be regular all the time although I never could understand why. Suppose you need a woman's touch around here."

Sid blushed and shifted down into the big stuffed armchair opposite her. He toyed with the piece of fabric covering the arm.

"Yes, well . . ."—he lifted his own glass—"cleaning women cost an arm and a leg these days." There was an awkward silence for a moment. "How long will you be staying?" He smiled at her. "I got plenty room."

"Now, Sid." Margaret winked. "Don't you go getting any funny ideas. I'll just be here the night. If I went home, Morley'd be at me with a straightjacket." She chuckled. "Poor Bertie. I'd hate to be around when he finds out."

"What about tomorrow night?" Sid opened the top collar button on his shirt and leaned back. "I mean if whatever it is you're planning doesn't work out."

Margaret picked up the magazine again. "It'll work out, then we'll all be back to normal. It's just tonight that I'm worried about."

Sid sighed and got up slowly. "I guess I'll put on the chicken. Creamed broccoli or carrots and peas?"

"Creamed broccoli. I'll make the salad."

Sid grinned. "Who said I had salad?"

"You men!" She shook her head and together they went out to the kitchen. On her way past, Margaret made sure the door was bolted on the inside.

The dinner was a real success. For the first time in years Sid set the dining-room table. First he had to remove all the curios and bric-a-brac that had found a resting place there, and in the process Margaret caught a glimpse of a woman's picture in a silver frame.

"Emma?" Margaret asked.

He smiled faintly and looked down at it. "We were up in the mountains one summer, just before she got sick. She wanted a picture so I would remember."

"She looks lovely."

"I would have remembered anyway, but I knew it would please her. Drove five miles before I could find a store that sold cameras. Those little Brownie box things." His smile thinned. "I suppose I still got it somewhere." He set the forks down and looked up at her. "I try not to think about her too much. Sometimes it's difficult."

"I know," Margaret sighed. "We all have our silver frames somewhere. I have Oscar up on the mantelpiece. But you can't always live in the past. It's not healthy and it's, well, boring, you know, to others. Not me that is, but . . ."

"You're right," Sid said. "In fact I've a confession. Last week I put an extra five down on a long shot. Paid off twenty to one." He came around and straightened a knife. "Horse was named Emma's Folly. I thought, what the hell—for old times' sake. If the old lady knew she'd tunnel another six feet down."

Margaret laughed. "That's it. No sense in being maudlin. Think the chicken's ready?"

"Better be. I'm starving."

They ate slowly, talking about old friends now gone and the changes they'd seen in the city. Sid made an attempt to find out about Margaret's involvement with the police, but all she said was that it was too complicated.

"It will be over tomorrow," she reassured him.

"That's good," Sid said. "Because you seem a little nervous tonight. Almost like you expect something to happen."

"Well, maybe I do," Margaret said. "Maybe I do."

40

"GODDAMNIT!" Morley hit the little table and sent the empty beef bouillon cup spinning. Bertie slipped another six inches down into the bed until the covers were over her nose. "Who the hell was on duty here anyway?" Morley raged. "Son-of-a-bitch oughta be busted. She waltzed right out."

"Don't blame Harelson," Schaeffer said. "He'd never seen her before."

"Christ! And now, this one won't talk?" He eyed Bertie with contempt.

Schaeffer nodded. "It's her friend Mrs. Mangione. She says she doesn't know where Margaret went to. We checked immediately at the garden, but no one was there. She's not at her apartment either."

"She doesn't know!" Morley took a step toward the bed. Bertie went completely under.

"No, Sam. I think she's telling the truth."

"What the hell!" Morley sat down heavily and let the roses he was holding fall to the floor. "Let her kill herself.

See if I care.'' He looked up slowly at Schaeffer. ''We lose the murderer, then we lose the stones. Last night it was almost Margaret's turn and we can't even keep her under protective custody. It's ridiculous. You try to do a job and she makes you feel like you're in a vaudeville routine. I should be directing a goddamn comedy here instead . . . except I'm maybe the only one that's not laughing.'' He lit a cigarette and looked over at the lump under the covers that was Bertie. ''Okay, tell her to beat it. The trouble with these old biddies is that you can't spank them. God knows it's what they deserve.''

He got up heavily and walked out of the room. Schaeffer followed. ''She'll call,'' Schaeffer said. ''She won't do it alone.''

''Let's hope so,'' Morley said. ''For her sake.'' He stomped off angrily down the hospital corridor.

41

THE phone rang as they were finishing their coffee. Sid made a movement to get it but Margaret held up her hand, moved quickly to the side, and lifted the receiver. She heard the sounds of heavy breathing and the noise of traffic in the background.

"Yes?"

"Margaret, is that you?"

"Vinnie?"

"Yes, listen." He spoke quickly. "I checked and I was right. Last night someone was in the garden and dropped something. I've got to show it to you. But it's gotta be right now. I think I'm being followed."

Margaret hesitated for just a second. She looked at Sid.

"Can you come over here? I'm with my friend."

"Yes, tell me where."

She gave him the address and name. "I'll tell the doorman to expect you."

"I'll be right there. . . . . Yeow!"

"What?" Margaret pressed the phone to her ear and thought she heard the sounds of a scuffle. Then the line went dead. She held the receiver in her hands for a few seconds, staring straight ahead. Slowly she put it back on its cradle.

"We're about to have a visitor," she told Sid. "At least I think we are."

Margaret began pacing up and down the living room, every now and then stopping in front of the window and peering down into the streets below. Sid made another pot of coffee and brought it into the room, but it didn't make the time go any faster. The minutes dragged by, the ashtray piled up with half-smoked cigarettes, and conversation was reduced to Margaret's asking for the time, first every fifteen minutes, then every five. An hour went by, then fifteen more minutes, one by one. Finally, the in-house phone rang and Sid picked it up. Margaret watched his face register confusion. His brow knitted and he rubbed the side of his nose slowly with his thumb. Then she saw his eyes open wide as he grasped the earpiece with both hands.

"What?" she demanded.

Sid straightened his shoulders, let the house phone dangle, and marched to the real phone in the living room. He dialed the three numbers, gave his address, and asked for an ambulance.

"For God's sake, what is it, Sid?"

"Your friend Vinnie just came in," he said, "with a four-inch knife in his side."

By the time they got downstairs Vinnie was unconscious and lying sprawled next to his radio near the front door. Margaret knelt over him and could see the knife sticking out three inches below his lowest rib on the left side. His face had several cuts and bruises and one of the pockets on his jacket was ripped open. He gave a low moan, but his eyes remained closed.

The doorman was doing his best to keep passersby at a distance, but once he saw Sid, he came over quickly. "I dunno . . ." He took his cap off and dragged a hand through his white hair. "He comes in holding his side and asks for you. Next thing I know he's on the floor. Jesus, Mr. Rossman, I didn't know what to do."

"It's okay, Fred, the ambulance will be here soon."

"He a friend of yours?"

"Yeah." Sid shrugged. "Sort of. You see anyone outside coulda done it?"

The doorman shook his head. "No one. Like I said, he just staggered in. I was by the table over there. When he fell I didn't think to look outside."

"Okay." Sid took a step closer and was about to kneel down next to Margaret when the piercing sound of the siren came through the heavy glass doors and stopped him. He went outside and brought the attendants in. Margaret was still on her knees next to the boy, looking carefully at his bruises.

The ambulance crew worked quickly. In five minutes Vinnie was strapped into the stretcher and on his way out. One of the attendants bent to pick up the radio.

"He going to make it?" Margaret asked him.

"Make it?" The attendant frowned. "Hell, we get at least a half dozen of these every weekend. Another month and this will be just a bad memory." He turned and helped with the stretcher. "It ain't too serious, but there's got to be a police report. See if you can check in tomorrow. Tonight, this kid needs some stitches and a lot of rest."

"He was going to tell us something," Sid said, without thinking. He looked quickly at Margaret.

"Yeah, well . . ." The attendant slammed the big rear door and started to move around to the driver's seat. "They all got a story."

42

MORLEY and Schaeffer rode up in the elevator in silence. As the doors were beginning to open, Schaeffer broke into Morley's thoughts. "I told you she'd call," he said.

Morley growled something inaudible and moved out into the well-lit corridor. Immediately the faintly astringent smell of the hospital hit them.

"What room?"

"The kid is in twelve-oh-three." They started walking. "Sam, she said this was it, the finale. Give her the chance."

"A judge ought to give her three to five as a public nuisance, that's what she deserves. If this is another of her little tea parties you're going to see a side of me you've never seen."

"The kid caught it on the way to give her some evidence. Should break it wide open."

"I don't know why you're so goddamned optimistic," Morley said. He stopped in front of a door. "Here we are."

"Christ, I haven't seen you this excited since Hobart got your promotion. Take it easy," Schaeffer cautioned.

"Cut it," Morley barked. "They're all in the kid's room, right?"

Schaeffer nodded. "She arranged it all this morning."

Together they turned into the room and drew back the curtains. There was a small circle of people sitting around Vinnie's bed. His face was bandaged in only a few spots and the side with the knife wound was propped up by a few extra pillows. Against the white of the sheets he managed to show a little color. He stared at the two policemen.

Margaret stood up. "I'm so glad you could come, Lieutenant. We've all recently arrived. I hope you don't mind the crowd."

"Not at all," he said, forcing himself to be polite. "And it's so nice to see you again, Margaret. Except the last time I recall you were in bed like your friend here." He nodded in the direction of Vinnie.

"Yes, well, *that* headache went away," said Margaret brightly. Then she caught herself. "Here, let me introduce everyone. These are the other gardeners. That's Cecile, John, Peter, and over by the window is Jerry. This is my friend Sid who was so kind as to put me up last night. And these two gentlemen," Margaret paused dramatically, "are Lieutenant Morley and Sergeant Schaeffer of the Eighty-first Precinct."

Morley nodded impatiently. "Let's get on with it then," he commanded.

Margaret's back stiffened. "I'm sure you realize, Lieutenant, what Vinnie's been through. I suggest we let him go at his own pace and tell us his story whichever way he sees fit."

"Sure, it's your ball game, Margaret," Morley snorted. "All the way to the showers."

"Your support is overwhelming." She smiled sarcastically. "There's a seat over by the window . . ."

"I'll stand if you don't mind," Morley said. He motioned to Schaeffer to wait by the door and he placed himself next to the side wall.

"Well, I think we're ready," Margaret announced. "Now, what was it you wanted to tell me last night, Vinnie? We're all waiting."

The boy struggled to raise himself a few inches in the bed and winced with the pain. He scratched his neck, took a sip of water, placed the glass back on the side table next to his radio, and began talking.

"Like I told you already, Margaret, there was something funny going on in the garden, right from the first. Doors left open, arguments, visitors at all times of the night. So I'm wondering what's so special about gardens and then it hit me. While we was planting all those nice vegetables and things, someone was using the place to grow pretty little weeds, the kind you smoke." A few of the kids stirred, but Vinnie went on. "But it wouldn't work, see. Luiz caught on and made the joker take it out. But he still had the seeds, so he figured why toss 'em, why not bury them in the garden, in a box or something until he can use them, maybe sometime later in the summer." Vinnie coughed and his hand went to clutch at his side. It took him a full minute before the pain passed and he caught his breath. "That's a lot of trouble to go through for a bunch of seeds, but the way I see it, these weren't just any seeds. They musta been special, African or Indonesian, maybe even Hawaiian, ones that couldn't be duplicated. And the street price for that stuff is outta sight." He smiled thinly. "Take my word." He scratched at his arm idly while he looked around. "So, like I said, I kinda guessed what was going down but I figure it's no big deal. After all, the seeds were already buried. Then, two nights ago, I just happen to be walking by the garden and sure enough, it's time for the guy to make his move. Of all things, Margaret's told us she's going to plant a tree right on top of his stash. He digs down and comes up with this little box. I'm watching as he lights a match to check to see it's still okay, and I guess he's satisfied because in no time he douses the match and beats it. I coulda followed, but I'm more curious about the garden. Besides, I think I recognize who it is anyway. I let myself in and there ain't nothing there 'cept this big hole, that and an empty book of matches." He smiled. "Well, I pocket them and don't think more about it until the next day . . . when Margaret says something about the cops about to close in on Luiz's murderer . . . and about how it's all related to the garden. Then I saw it plain as day. This midnight gardener is also the guy that offed Luiz, maybe when Luiz told him to take the dope out of the garden. Must've been in a moment of anger 'cause why else would someone kill for a box of seeds." He stopped suddenly and looked around.

"Go ahead," Morley said. "What happened then?"

"I remembered the matchbook. It had this kind of funny initial on it, and I thought I recognized it. That's when I told Margaret I had to check on something. And goddamn if I wasn't right. It took me a few hours, but I got a good memory and tracked it down. Here . . ." He scratched his shoulder for a second, leaned over, and opened the night table drawer. His hand fumbled, then came out holding two matchbooks. "This is the one I found in the garden." He flipped it onto the center of the bed and everyone leaned forward. Scrawled in a bold script on the front cover were two letters, "GC." Vinnie opened his hand again and showed an identical book, this one completely full.

"I got this one last evening," he said slowly and turned toward the window, "at Game City."

It was only because everyone turned toward Jerry at the same time that Morley had any idea what Vinnie's disclosure meant. Morley took a step closer to Jerry and waited.

Jerry's eyes opened to the size of rock oysters and his hand closed around the window latch. "That's a goddamn lie," he yelled. "I was never in the garden that night."

"Hold it." Morley clamped a hand on Jerry's shoulder. "Let him finish."

"Yeah," Vinnie said, "Game City, Jerry's second home. I knew then who killed Luiz. It was just a matter of telling Margaret. She said she had a cop friend. I called from a phone booth but I guess Jerry second-guessed me. He must have followed me from Game City. I was just hanging up when I felt this hand on my arm." He pointed to the spot, and as he did he gave it a hard scratch. "Christ, I was scared, so I ran as fast as I could. It was Jerry, I'm pretty sure. I pushed him over on the way out of the booth and I didn't look back. I guess I lost him in a couple of blocks, but I waited just the same. I was thinking of going uptown and getting some of my buddies in The Stallions to help, but it was getting late and there was no telling where they'd be. So's I just took the long way around to where Margaret was. Stupid of me. I shoulda known he woulda been waiting. I passed this alley and before I knew it there was this pain in my side and someone's kneeing me in the face. Son-of-a-bitch fights like an animal, worse than any of the guys up on 111th. It was over in a minute. He must have seen the knife in me and figured I'd had it. I heard him run away and somehow I managed to get up. I guess I staggered to Margaret's. Don't remember too much except holding on to that matchbook. Next thing I knew, here I am." He smiled thinly at them. "And that's it." He sank back into the pillows. "Jerry's your murderer, the little bastard."

Jerry shouted and before anyone could do anything he was at the bed. He drew his fist back but Schaeffer caught it with his good arm and spun him around.

"Easy, tiger." Schaeffer pinned his arm in a hammerlock but Jerry continued to struggle. The boy's face turned a pale crimson and his hair flew down over his forehead. He tried to wrench free but Schaeffer had too good a grip.

"Son-of-a-bitch! I didn't kill anyone," Jerry panted, "just 'cause I wouldn't cut you in."

Everyone started shouting. Out of the general melee that ensued, Margaret's voice was finally heard.

"It's no use struggling, Jerry. Sergeant Schaeffer's too strong. If you relax we can continue." It took another few seconds, but Jerry finally stopped moving and slumped in Schaeffer's grip.

"That's better," the policeman said and started reaching for his set of cuffs.

"Oh, no, David, not yet," Margaret pleaded. "Unless you want to arrest him for the attempted cultivation of a few little weeds which in fact never really got started. No, Jerry's not the murderer. He couldn't possibly be."

"Huh?" Now it was Morley's turn. "Why not?"

Margaret took a deep breath and turned around. From where she was standing by the side of the bed, she could see everyone.

"Well, it's true. Jerry did try to grow some marijuana in the garden. Luiz found out about it a little while later on his own. He must have recognized the little shoots and asked Jerry to take them out. They had an argument which Vinnie overheard and then demanded to be cut in. Jerry refused and decided with all that was going on, he'd better take the plants out. That was done late one night after the police reopened the garden. My friend Rose happened to see Jerry in the process. But Luiz wasn't killed on account of that." She looked at Morley. "I'm surprised at you, Lieutenant. Don't let all this commotion confuse you. Don't forget the diamonds. That's what was in the box, not marijuana seeds. No, this whole issue is just a blind. We mustn't forget what the murderer was after."

They all looked at each other but Sid was the first to say it: "Diamonds?"

"Yes," Margaret continued. "The Rosenblatt diamonds." She waited patiently until the noise quieted down. "And the first real clue to the murderer came from Mr. Rosenblatt himself. When I visited him he said something very peculiar. He said that he was sure there was only one person involved in the holdup, but that when he was on the ground, just before blacking out, he had the impression there were two people. Now that's very unusual, especially since he claimed he could only see one pair of sneakers. Well, there's only one way you can get that impression." She smiled at Morley, "And that is if someone is wearing two different color socks." She let that sink in for a minute, then continued. "I would have filed that away as just a peculiarity except that I remembered something else, something that I saw at Luiz's apartment. And that," she said, "was a bottle of Thunderbird wine."

Schaeffer interrupted. "That was in Gondolpho's report. Except he had it as filled with dishwashing fluid."

"Precisely. Green fluid. The same that was sprayed, or should I say, spit, against the wall. You see, Luiz was always borrowing things, and just by chance he put some borrowed soap in an empty bottle of Thunderbird wine, a bottle that should have normally contained a red wine. The murderer must have seen the bottle by the sink after the crime and taken a swallow to calm his nerves, a quite natural response. Except, only one kind of person could have made that mistake. The same kind of person who puts on two different color socks. Someone who is color blind."

"Very clever," Morley grunted, "but it was still a guess."

"Why certainly," Margaret continued. "Everything starts with a guess. In any case, I set out to test this premise, to find if any of the helpers happened to be color blind. You remember, Peter, I visited you at the factory and found you in the middle of dozens of racks of dresses, all in different colors. I watched while you got a delivery together, six of one color, twelve of another and so forth, and I knew it couldn't be you.''

"Of course not," Peter said. "I got the best eyes in the business. I could tell you the difference between a mauve and a lavender from fifty feet."

"Exactly. So that afternoon I went to visit John at his air-conditioning school and I found him in the midst of what looked like an electronic spaghetti factory. Hundreds of different parts with all kinds of colored wires sticking out. What was that one I held up?''

John thought for a minute. "You mean the thermostat?"

"Yes, that's it. Now if John were color blind, I'm sure he would have electrocuted himself by then, so he was eliminated and that left Jerry, Cecile, and Vinnie."

Jerry stood up straighter, but Schaeffer's hand was still on his arm. His face had gone back to its normal color. "Well, it couldn't be me," he said. "You know very well . . .''

"I do," Margaret smiled. "That three in the side pocket. No, you can't play pool if you're color blind unless you ask a lot of questions. The way you were punching those balls in order into those pockets, it couldn't have been you.''

Morley frowned. "Then it must be Cecile."

"Possibly. Of course, it was quite unlikely. I had remembered reading something about color blindness and its relative infrequency amongst women. So I checked at the library, and while the incidence is less than one hundredth of that in men, I couldn't count Cecile out. That's when I told you, David, that I had narrowed it down to two.''

"I remember." Inadvertently, he let go of his grip on Jerry's arm.

"Well, I tried with each one, but unlike the others, there

was no way I could eliminate either one.'' She paused.
''That is, until we did our first harvest. Then it became obvious. Everyone except the murderer managed to pick only the ripe tomatoes. There wasn't one green tomato in any bag except for yours''—she turned—''Vinnie, and yours was full of them. I remembered my friend Bertie even commenting on it.''

Vinnie sat up and lowered the hand with which he had been scratching his shoulder. ''So, I like green tomatoes,'' he snarled. ''What's it to you? You gonna convince a judge I murdered someone on account of a green salad?'' He managed a dry laugh.

''He's right,'' Morley said. ''And what about the attack last night?''

''What attack?'' Margaret looked down at Vinnie. ''There were so many holes in that story you could drive a one-oh-four bus through it. He's the only one that knew I was at Sid's. No one was waiting for him. It's quite clear. He stabbed himself.'' She frowned and shook her head. ''You've got to understand who we're dealing with, Lieutenant. Vinnie knew I was close to figuring it out and tried to kill me twice.''

''Twice!'' Morley stepped forward. ''Twice?''

Margaret passed it off with a wave of her hand. ''A minor thing. Just a good recipe with bad ingredients. I didn't think you'd be interested.''

''You didn't think . . .''

''It doesn't matter,'' Margaret continued smoothly. ''Now this person was desperate, and ruthless, and certainly not above faking an attack if it could shift the blame. He knew from my questions that I suspected one of the helpers, so right from the beginning he tried to implicate Jerry and weave the story around what he remembered, Jerry's fairly innocent marijuana fiasco.'' She pointed a finger at Vinnie. ''That thing with the matchbooks was very dramatic, I'll grant you, but quite pointless nonetheless.'' She took a deep breath. ''This is getting a little tiring. Lieutenant, could I have one of your cigarettes?''

Morley patted his pockets until he came up with the pack. He leaned over and handed her one, but his eyes were on the boy in the bed.

''Thank you.'' She lit the cigarette and inhaled deeply. ''There, that's better.'' She took another puff before continuing. ''No, Lieutenant, we're dealing with a real cool customer here, someone who had the determination and courage to stick a knife in his own side if it meant getting away with a murder; the same kind of person, I might add, who could burn himself with a cigarette lighter just to impress a bunch of friends with how fearless he was, the same friends, I suspect, he was trying to impress with his solo robbery. What about it, Vinnie?''

Vinnie stopped scratching his elbow for a moment and covered the scar on his wrist. There was an uneasy silence in the room for a few seconds. Then Vinnie uncovered his wrist and pointed a finger at Margaret.

''Yeah, what proof have you got?''

''Well, of course, that's the problem. The stones are gone. That was a serious mistake. I did however anticipate that some such turn of events might develop and prepared, just in case.'' She turned to Schaeffer. ''I'm sorry, David. It's not that I didn't trust you. I just had to make sure.''

''Thanks.'' He frowned.

''So''—she turned back—''I figured if he wouldn't leave us with any identifying prints or marks, we'd leave some with him. Actually, it was kind of unfair. I took advantage of the fact that you're all city kids and have no real experience outside city streets. I mean in the woods.'' She smiled. ''And I guess I was right, because none of you realized that what I had planted over the box of stones, that low ground creeper, was nothing other than good old-fashioned poison ivy.''

Vinnie's hand stopped scratching his elbow and he looked at her in anger.

"No, go ahead, Vinnie, and scratch. I see you've got it all over your neck too. Pity. And you're the only one with it too." She looked around. "Of course it was difficult keeping you all away from it, but you see, I couldn't let anyone else get it. Jerry almost foiled me when he tried to get his cucumbers. It was the only sure sign of guilt if the stones disappeared. The way I figure it, it's probably the only patch of poison ivy in all of Manhattan. That's why I had to wait a couple of days after the stones were dug up, Lieutenant, to give it a chance to develop."

Sid interrupted. "So that's why you wanted the car. I couldn't figure it."

Margaret nodded and crushed out the cigarette. "Yes, it's not exactly the kind of thing you can order from your neighborhood nursery." She looked down at the boy in the bed, now scratching uncontrollably at his neck. "It's quite something if you've never had it. I remember one summer, Oscar and I were up near Oswego . . ."

"I'm sorry, Margaret." Morley came forward and stood right next to the bed. "It's a good trick. I mean, we all know you're right. The kid took the stones, murdered Luiz, but it's not enough. Not these days. We gotta deal with real judges and defense attorneys and I guarantee the D.A. wouldn't touch a case with that kind of proof. They'd laugh us right out of court. So the kid's color blind, there are thousands of them in the city. And as far as the itchies are concerned, there's no saying Vinnie didn't take a bus out to the country one day on an innocent little picnic."

"That's right," Vinnie said smugly. "Me and my friend Sal, president of The Stallions." He let that sink in for a moment. "Zampino sandwiches and beer." He chuckled. "Now where you going, old lady? That's it. The showers, as your friend here said."

Schaeffer made a move toward the bed but Morley held him back.

"You mean what I've found is not enough?" Margaret was surprised. "The poison ivy's a clear mark of guilt. No one else got it."

"I'm afraid not, Margaret," Morley said. "It is not good enough on its own. We need some hard evidence, like the stones. Without them, we don't have a case."

"Stones? What stones?" Vinnie asked. "Maybe the Rolling Stones? I got them on tape."

"The only thing we can do is get a warrant," Morley continued. "Maybe if we're lucky . . ."

"You won't find them," Margaret said slowly. "At least not where he lives. He's too careful for that." She frowned and looked off to a corner of the room. For a moment she was lost in thought.

Morley cut through the quiet. "Well, we can try, and right now." He got up to go. "There's nothing more we can do here."

"Wait a minute." Margaret held up her hand. "Maybe there is." She looked down at Vinnie.

"You know, it's funny," she said. "I'm always surprised when people change habits abruptly. Do things that they've never done, or on the other hand, avoid things that they always do. Little inconsistencies like that, there's usually some reason for it." She looked at Vinnie again and now he was beginning to perspire. "Something like that's been bothering me for the last few days. Nothing I could put my finger on until now. And of course it's always harder when it's the absence of something rather than vice versa."

"What are you getting at, Margaret?" Schaeffer was genuinely puzzled. "Absence of what?"

"Noise, music, disco, or whatever it is Vinnie's always listening to. I noticed it yesterday in the garden while we were planting the tree. Vinnie had his radio with him, but not once did he turn it on. That was very unusual.'' She got up and slowly made her way around the bed. On the night table, partially hidden by the water pitcher and the lamp, was his radio. She pulled it out. ''And here it is. He even had it with him last night. It was almost like a piece of clothing with him. I don't think I've ever seen him without it.'' Margaret stared accusingly at Vinnie. ''And yet, before the police came to the hospital today, while we were waiting for everyone, the radio was silent again. Two days, and not one note. Now why is that, Vinnie?''

The boy was mute. The perspiration made the poison ivy on his neck glint in little wet oily patches.

''Because, I'm tired of it,'' he answered at last.

''Is that why, Vinnie?'' She smiled and placed her finger on the On button. ''Or is it because there are no batteries in it? This is a big radio, Vinnie. I'm sure it takes a lot of batteries. In some kind of battery pack, right?'' She moved her finger. Everyone heard the click, but nothing else came out of it. No music, no static, nothing.

''Of course, I could be wrong. Maybe the batteries are just dead. In which case''—she moved her hand—''they should be replaced.'' In one quick motion she touched another button and a little door flew open. Like a gopher peering out of a hole, a square cartridge jumped up and rested on the edge of the radio.

''Imagine that,'' she said with a chuckle. She looked down at the glint of reflected light coming from inside the cartridge. ''I've heard of single crystal radios, but this is ridiculous.''

43

"OH, there you are," Margaret said, poking her head around the doorway. "I came by to give you some of my latest cookies." She opened the door farther and walked into Morley's office. "Bertie's with me, I hope you don't mind?"

"Not at all." Morley smiled and stood up. "Have a seat."

The two women made themselves comfortable across from the lieutenant and Margaret placed a cardboard box on his desk. "Vanilla-pecan," she said. "Baked them last night."

"I thought you'd relax after all that activity in the hospital yesterday." Morley grinned. "That was quite a performance." He leaned back in his chair. "How long had you known the diamonds were in the radio?"

"I didn't." She grinned. "Just a lucky guess. Were they all there?"

"Every last one. You should have seen the expression on Rosenblatt's face when I showed him."

"Well, I knew it was Vinnie all along," Bertie said. "There was never a doubt in my mind."

Morley lifted the top of the box and took out one of the cookies. "Gondolpho's taking over, Margaret," he said after finishing the cookie. "He doesn't think there'll be any problem with the D.A. From here on it's open and shut, thanks to you."

"And Bertie," Margaret added. "She helped a lot."

"I still don't understand how." Her friend blushed. "You wouldn't tell me a thing."

Margaret looked at Morley with a twinkle in her eye. "Sometimes," she said, "not knowing is safer." She got up to go. "Well, I hope you like those cookies, Samuel. I can bring some others next week." She raised her eyebrows hopefully.

"I'll look forward to that. Not having you around the station house is going to make this job awfully dull. Besides"— he held up another cookie—"I like your recipes."

"Oh, my," Margaret said. "That reminds me." She fumbled in her bag for a moment and brought out another package, this one wrapped in aluminum foil. "You did say you were interested . . ."

"What . . ." He pulled it closer.

"Just another bit of bakery," she said. "Unfortunately quite indigestible. If you have your lab check it I think they'll find it's full of Malathion." She smiled. "The first of Vinnie's little tricks." She turned to go. "Good-bye, Lieutenant, see you next week. Come on, Bertie, before the benches fill up." The two women shuffled out. The last thing Margaret saw before closing the door was Morley staring at the aluminum-foil package in one of his hands. In his other hand was one of Margaret's vanilla-pecan cookies, waiting to be eaten.